131

DIFFERENT

THINGS

131

PAPL
DISCARDED

DIFFERENT

THINGS

BY
ZACHARY LIPEZ
NICK ZINNER +
STACY WAKEFIELD

BROOKLYN, NEW YORK, USA
BALLYDEHOB, CO. CORK, IRELAND

NOVELLA BY
ZACHARY LIPEZ

PHOTOS BY
NICK ZINNER

BOOK BY
STACY WAKEFIELD

1 NEW YORK 2004
2-3 BERLIN 2003
4 NEW YORK 1999
5-8 NEW YORK 2001
9 TOKYO 2013
10 CHARLESTON, SC 1999

TEN
PLACES
WE HAD
A DRINK
TOGETHER

2

1   3

4

7

8

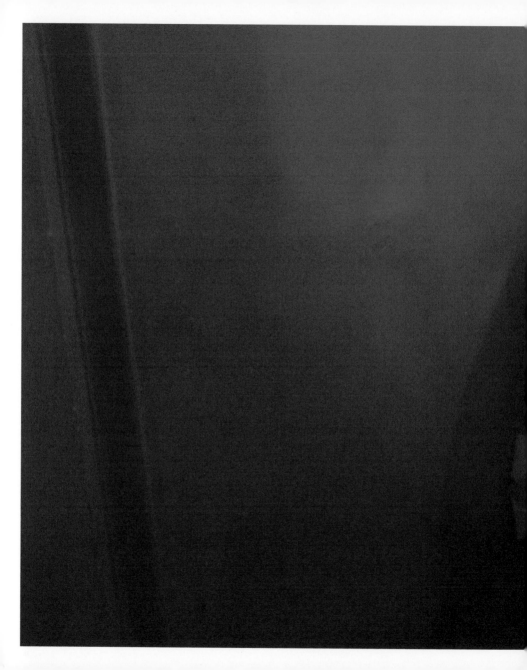

SEVEN BARS
ONE NIGHTCLUB
ONE LOFT
& A DINER

At 12:03 Saturday afternoon the phone in my pocket started vibrating. I didn't need to pull it out to know it was the regulars calling because the gates to Pym's Cup were still down. I was a block away. That was fine. They wouldn't call the owner till twelve fifteen. They didn't want to snitch on someone who had control of their noontime drink unless it was absolutely necessary.

When he saw me coming, Caldwell Teenager put down the receiver on the last working pay phone in the tristate area. He pulled a loosie out of the change dispenser and relit it. His hands trembled, but only a little.

"I just wanted to make sure you were okay. Are you okay?"

"I'm fine, Caldwell. Thank you."

I undid the padlocks at each side of the gate, throwing them one by one in front of the entrance. Even though I didn't need it, Caldwell helped me lift the gates.

The art on the wall was renewed on a regular basis. We'd had a dinosaur giving a cop the finger, a riot cop eating a cartoonish still-squealing BLT, *I Miss Giuliani* in sharp angular letters, and, of course, *RIP* . . . whatever. NYC, LES, Democracy. The current mural was Uncle Sam felating a skeletal camel with dollar signs dripping from his chin.

I put the book of skateboarding photography I'd been making a show of looking at on the train behind the register, cover peeking out. I glanced at my phone as I ran the dishwater to clean the glasses that the nighttime bartender had left. My phone, habitually dropped, was on its last legs, with nothing on the inside screen but Sanskrit, though the outer notifications told me that there were six missed calls that I'd failed to notice as I ran from the J/M/Z station. Caldwell Teenager (from the sidewalk pay phone, twice), Steve, Young Steve, Terry the Faggot, and Whitey. The other four must have gone to get coffee for their beers. They arrived en masse as I came out from the quixotic task of sort of cleaning the bathrooms.

"Any bodies in there?" Young Steve called out from the doorway.

Everyone laughed like it was the first time they'd heard that joke.

The regulars all drink beer at first, so I gave them all beer. I wiped down the bar with a damp rag. Someone put on the Monkees' "Stepping Stone" three times in a row when I had my back turned. The regulars yelled at each other and no one fessed up and we all sang along for the third run.

There was change on the bar for my tips. I didn't fling change off the bar till the evening.

Steve sat with Young Steve—who was a few years older than Steve but had been hanging out at Pym's for a shorter time—in the corner by the lone large multi-paned window. The panes were all different colors, replaced on the cheap as they got punched in. The sun managed to get through the cracks and graffiti and the Steves were convinced it made day drinking tropical. Whitey, a black Dominican born and bred on Avenue D, sat underneath the *Absolutely No Card Playing* sign that he, through bad luck and worse temper, had been the cause of. Caldwell Teenager, in his thirties looking fifty, stood next to him, leaning on the *Addams Family* pinball machine. Its top glass was cracked but it still worked, emitting the theme song every few minutes. In several hours these guys would sing along to that too. Terry the Faggot, not gay just not great at sticking up for himself, sat a little farther away, hunched in his trenchcoat, unsure if everyone was his friend today or not. I put half a shot of vodka in front of him. He'd been hassled pretty bad on my last shift. Everyone had taken ice cubes out of his rum and Coke to throw at him because he "didn't really care much for *Die Hard*." It was hard to defend. He always said shit like that. Just thinking about it, I wanted to take the vodka back.

At one thirty, my former wife came in. She was dragging some twentysomething coke vulture with her. She looked okay, half-Cuban/half-Irish and all that went with that (strikingly good looks till death, counterintuitively racist parents), but the dude with her was wearing a black leather jacket with, god help us all, no shirt underneath. It was thirty degrees outside. I poured myself a half pint.

"Good morning, Sam."

Aviva hoisted an oversized black purse, fringed with silver studs and something clanging inside, onto the bar. She pushed it toward me. I put it behind the bar.

"I'll have a margarita, no salt, extra ice, it's early, and my boo here will have a beer. Do you care what kind, boo?"

"Whatever's clever."

I gave Aviva a look. She arched an eyebrow. I made her margarita weak.

Aviva managed the art factory for one of those ceramic monstrosity pop artists who didn't disappear after the eighties, making sure the thirty passive-aggressive dudes she outranked painted enough silver circles and oversized ceramic doll parts to make the artist another twenty million.

When we'd gotten married, I still had a camera and was still naïve enough to think I had the talent to become the next Spike Jonze if Spike Jonze had quit or died before he made movies. Back then, Aviva was wild all the time and that was what I liked; she gave me action to document. But truth was, I was only dinking around; after some early success with my skateboarding shots, I never found another subject I could sink my teeth into, and when Aviva got bored of partying and focused on work, she turned out to have a lot of talent. She'd made a solid career, while I had given up trying. By the end, I was borrowing money from her all the time and resenting her for it. And when we broke up things only got worse. I didn't even have a darkroom anymore and was too much of a curmudgeon to switch to digital. My only goal for my bartending career was to be like the ones in books or *After Hours*; the sort who didn't hand out wisdom, didn't flirt, but who grizzled regulars called "nurse."

I gave her date—who looked like both the singer of the Dead Boys and a literal dead boy—a Bud Light. Fuck that guy.

"Sam, this margarita is not your best. I'm not mad, as I'm not paying for it, but I think you should know."

"Thank you, Aviva. I like your necklace."

Aviva's silver-and-turquoise multitiered chest piece descended into her bosom. She was leaning into the bar to accentuate it. I knew better than to think it was for my benefit. It was just the way she leaned into bars. She was five feet something, I guess plus-sized if we're siding with the patriarchy. Hot by human standards, if no longer my type. She draped herself in layers of shawls and scarfs that always managed to shift off her shoulder and still stay on, held together by occult brooches and pins of German industrial bands. Her black hair was pulled high on the top and struggling to get free. I was thinking if she took the compliment well, and it seemed like things were okay, that I would show her my picture in the skateboarding book. I wanted to think she could still be proud of me.

"Do you know who got this necklace for me, Sam?"

"This guy?" I pointed to Stiv Shirtless, whose chin had fallen into his chest. Maybe on a nod, but maybe simply a coke-just-wore-off-no-sleep-and-now-it's-the-afternoon prebrunch nap.

"No, Sam. *You* did. On our anniversary. Our first and only anniversary. You thought I didn't notice that you'd forgotten, if you even ever knew the date, and you ran to some marked-up Tibet shop and bought me half a dozen necklaces. Did you even look at them?"

"I was just messing around. Of course I remember it. You look very nice."

"Get fucked, Sam. I bought it last year on MacDougal. You gave me a bottle of Patrón. Then you disappeared up that slut's cunt."

"Ah."

Aviva slammed down her empty glass and got up. She saw the photography book behind me and her tone softened: "Sorry if I'm snippy. I've been working sixty-hour weeks at the studio. Now I have a few days off, what with the holiday weekend. I'm gonna work some stuff out. Deduct what I'd normally tip a human being from the money you owe me."

"Will do. Thanks for coming by."

She flipped me off and grabbed "boo" by the hair. He followed her out the bar bent over. I hoped their brunch would be overpriced.

It had been crazy to think she'd be interested in the book. I'd submitted my photos when we'd still been together. I liked to think I'd gotten in on my own, but I figured maybe she'd made some calls. I didn't want to get into who owed what to who. I was pretty sure that ledger might sting. Whatever. I'd done plenty for her too. Plenty for lots of people. My friend Francis always said, "It's not a favor if they expect gratitude."

Everyone came to Pym's prebrunch. A prebrunch drink gave you the courage to face the miserable staff and hungover crowds. It was less problematic than drinking at home before you went out to drink over twelve-dollar eggs.

I sipped a PBR. The long shift loomed ahead of me. I'd be here till eight if the swing-shift bartender showed, ten if he didn't. I didn't want him to. Money was tight and they'd just raised my Bushwick rent. I'd already been forced out of Williamsburg and, in counterintuitive order, Manhattan (which, before Vicki, I'd never thought I'd live in). I could use an extra fifty dollars. I didn't mind the hours. A lot of bartenders got into it for short hours and fast money, but bartending wasn't a stepping stone to something better for me. It was a calling of sorts, bellowing and insistent, in that I was good enough at it that I'd only get fired if I tried, or stole more than what I gave away or drank myself. And traditional third-round buybacks—while being phased out citywide because of high bar rent and just not enough patrons who deserved them—were not a firing offense in the places I worked. My boss screamed at us to not buy the regulars drinks but didn't mean it in the slightest. Anyway, I'd been told that my dad had owned a bar in New Brunswick before I'd been born or, hell, maybe after I'd been born, so I figured it was in my thinning blood.

By four I had to ask both the Steves to leave. They were arguing about Iggy and the Stooges and playing "Raw Power" on repeat to bolster their positions on Bowie's negative or positive influence. A good jukebox can ruin a bartender's favorite bands. By play eight, I turned off the music, removed their drinks from the bar, and said, "See you tomorrow, gentlemen." Eventually they stopped hurling obscenities and left, presumably to go three blocks east to the Library, where they refused to accept that they had been 86'd for at least a year. I had to return their $3.75 in tips but it was worth it. As soon as they left, Terry the Faggot stumbled over to the jukebox and played "Raw Power."

The after-brunch crowd came in, a mixture of regulars, barely legal punks/skins trying on day drinking to see how it fit, and the inevitable slumming grad students, with their need to collect characters. We were a dive bar but a well-located one. Business was brisk. I worked fast, pouring drafts, laughing at mojito requests, showing people who called me "chief" the door. I answered to "man" and "yo." Rules with low stakes are still rules.

I threw Whitey out at five for snoring too loud and Caldwell Teenager threw himself out when I walked in his direction after he grabbed a college girl's ass. The first wave was replaced by the second. Murray and Drunk Fireman took over the regulars' corner and ordered shots.

Sanita and Sarita came in at five thirty. They weren't sisters but they could have been extras in the same version of *Cleopatra*. They were full-figured, big-boned, good to look at, with matching black Bettie Page bangs, heavy eyeliner, and lots of black lace. Murray and Drunk Fireman hooted when they came in. Drunk Fireman lumbered to the jukebox to play the Smiths to impress Sarita. I put up two strong vodka tonics with extra limes and minimal ice. Neither girl put any money down.

"Thanks, Saaaaaam," Sanita and Sarita said in unison.

They vibed a couple smaller girls out of their barstools and got comfortable, building a fortress with their drinks and purses.

I was going to tell them that Aviva had been by but I thought better of it. Discussion of other females with Sanita and Sarita sometimes took a turn. They were Aviva fans for the most part, sometimes in ways that made me feel judged, but I made no pretense of understanding the friendships of women.

Sanita beat me to it: "So, Sam. We saw your lady."

"Aviva? Not my lady. You girls are my ladies now, uh, ladies."

"No, Sam. Your OTHER girl."

My stomach did a thing. I looked to the bathroom out of habit. It would be disastrous to get sick. I had bad acid reflux to the point of social anxiety. My time spent in the bathroom was noted. I made people late for things. I made myself late worrying about making people late. Occasionally there was blood in the bowl. One of the reasons me and Francis, my best friend, bonded in high school was that he could get Nexium as well as pot back when you needed a prescription for the antacid and the idea of prescription pot was laughable. But taking a shit at Pym's was out of the question. The bathroom doors had no locks. The owner had had them removed to facilitate the removal of fornicators and ODs.

I sweat a little from the forehead for a variety of reasons.

"Really."

"Yep. Vicki. Large as life and twice as stuck up. Sorry. I mean *super nice*." Sanita forced down a lime wedge with her straw. Sarita looked embarrassed and sent her smile in the direction of Drunk Fireman. He beamed at her.

Sanita snickered at the look on my face. "Oh, Sam. Calm down. I'm sorry I said anything. You have customers."

Happy hour was in full swing. I ignored those waving money and served those trying to get my attention through force of will. I saw everyone, despite what they thought. There was a hierarchy based on customers' grasp of etiquette.

The skinhead contingent was growing. That was a concern but not an issue yet. There were still plenty of other tough guys in the bar and the presence of Drunk Fireman, who was both enormous and a profound nonappreciator of subculture nuances, gave me comfort. Anyway, neither Flannery nor Big Timmy were there and they were the real problems.

I wanted to get back to Sanita and Sarita and hear more. First Aviva coming through and now the mention of Vicki, my one true love, ender of marriages and my heart. My stomach wanted to do a Pee Wee Herman on the bar. (His dance from the movie, not the unjustly maligned jacking off.)

One of the skinheads, bless his dummy heart, distracted me by playing the one Skrewdriver song on the jukebox. It was on a mix CD that a former bartender had allowed when she was sleeping with one of the skins. It was from Skrewdriver's first album, which was technically nonracist. But technically nonracist in skinhead terms just meant a wider range of peoples to hate and perform violence upon. I pressed the skip button hidden under the bar and yelled, "Someone must have bumped the machine!" There was shouting from the skins but laughter from Drunk Fireman and from Murray, who was friends with the owner and reputed to have killed a couple guys in the eighties, so that was that. I made kamikaze shots to placate all sides. Many tattooed hands were raised in cheers.

"Up with us, down with them."

I collected tips off the bar and put them in the jar by the iron register. I rang some of the free-drink tips in to keep the ring up. I liked to ring at least a thousand per shift as a personal challenge. The old-fashioned register made a reassuring clang and bang that soothed my stomach. I turned back to Sanita and Sarita.

"I can't handle games, Sanita. I'm fragile. Please say what you're saying."

"Sam. It was nothing. I shouldn't have said anything. It's just . . ."

She drew on her vodka tonic until it made a sucking noise. She giggled and held the glass out. Sarita did the same. I looked down their shirts. They owed me that much.

"We'll tell you all about it when Francis gets here. He should hear this too. In the meantime, you have too many buttons buttoned." Sanita leaned over the bar and unbuttoned my top two buttons and I let her. She tucked in my shirt, pausing for a second over my waist. Goth girls were particular about men and button-downs. One down was strictly Wall Street. All the way up you were a Nazi or a wizard. Three down you looked like a Bad Seed. Sanita had nice hands. I refilled their drinks.

As if on cue, Francis, my aforementioned best friend and that night's swing-shift bartender, walked in with Virgil, the night-shift bartender who was also my friend, and who I had referred to as my "token black friend" until he slammed me against a wall and explained how entirely offensive he found that.

Virgil shook my hand; he'd refused to give me complicated handshakes since our altercation. He went to the back room to hide his skateboard and change his shirt. Francis kissed the girls for too long on the cheek and grinned at me, arms outstretched. He didn't care if I hugged him. It was just a greeting.

"Francis. Hello. Do you want to work your swing shift?"

"Sam. I do not."

"Good. What are you drinking?"

"Nothing for now. I need to talk to these fine bitches. Ladies? My office?"

The girls slid off their stools and followed Francis outside to smoke. I saw them through the window both offer Francis cigarettes. He took both, tucking one behind his ear and lighting the other from Sanita's lit one. When he leaned in, Sarita leaned in too even though she didn't need to.

Some frat boys at the west side of the bar were calling out for Irish Car Bombs. I made the drinks and charged an extra dollar for the effort and another for the corniness.

Outside, Francis was making jokes and the ladies were laughing. Sanita smacked Francis so his winter cap fell preciously in his eyes. Sarita fixed it, kissing him on the cheek.

When they came back in, Francis still had lipstick on his face until he noticed Drunk Fireman giving him a hard look, and he scrubbed it off fast.

There was a lull in the orders. Virgil, though he wasn't due to work for two hours, started cleaning glasses and setting them to dry in front of the top-shelf liquor. I took the opportunity to show off the book. I opened to a page in the middle, with a black-

and-white photo of Virgil in his glory, shirtless and in full flight over a passed-out oogle.

"Well, damn. There I am! Nice! I like the way you caught sleeping beauty. Took me three tries to get the landing right. Those train punks are real sound sleepers."

Francis, who'd gotten my excited call when the book arrived at my door, made exaggerated motions of needing a drink. I knew he was proud of me getting something published, but as I hadn't gotten paid, it still sort of figured into his image of me as the world's dope for the kicking.

I dropped the book behind the register and gave Francis a Guinness and a shot of Jameson. He put a twenty on the bar and I ignored it. It was the same twenty that had passed from bartender to bartender since times immemorial. The joke I'd heard since I was old enough to change a keg was that there was one solitary twenty-dollar bill in New York City, shared amongst all bar staff. Nobody rang it in and it went from tip jar to tip jar, never to find rest till Bartender Jesus returned.

Sanita and Sarita went to the bathroom together, Pym's Cup being one of those bars where that was absolutely required for ladies. Someone had to watch the door at all times.

Francis did his shot. He took off his hat and set it by his beer. He looked like a River Phoenix who'd lived, but not necessarily well. He was still devastatingly handsome. His hair did things I could never get pomade to approximate. At thirty-three, wear was setting in. Men, in general, get more handsome with age, but there's a certain kind of elfishness that hints at serious future disappointment with every crow's foot around the eyes. Women still forgave Francis anything and everything, so it was possible that my having known him in his aesthetic purity put me in the minority of seeing lines of doom come off him. I still liked looking at him, though. He tapped his shot glass and I refilled it. We had a moment.

"Sam. I apparently have to talk to you about Vicki."

"Okay."

"She's back in town."

"Okay." I started to sweat again.

"That's not all."

"O-KAY."

"Vicki is, from what the fat furies—no disrespect—are telling me, drinking again. Admittedly, the ladies are only occasionally dependable sources. But I choose to believe them."

I heard the sound of angels, though it may have been the Cocteau Twins, coming from the jukebox. I turned it up.

Francis looked concerned. "See, that face you're making concerns me. The fact that you just turned up this awful music concerns me. I told Sanita and Sarita that I didn't want to tell you and they insisted. They love drama. They love it. Are you going enable them, Sam?"

I heard choral hymns and the lights above me flickered. I spit up into the trash can next to me. I poured myself my first shot of the night. Jameson. Just a single. I had to keep my wits about me.

"We have to find her."

"Oh, Sam. Please no. I just want to get drunk. I just want to get drunk with my friend and I want to get some pussy and I want to ditch my friend for said pussy."

"We have to find her."

"Sam. I'm begging you. So she's drinking. So what? That means nothing. I want to have a fun Saturday. No missions. No romance. No Vicki."

But if Vicki was drinking again, then Vicki could love me again.

I really missed Vicki and I hadn't cum in a really good way for as long as I could remember. I was tired of being drunk all the time, staring at chests on the subway, getting home to my one-bedroom with a closet I was forced to rent out, locking my door, masturbating to a combination of free Internet porn, my memories of people who'd allowed me to cum on their faces, and whatever chestal imagery I'd managed to collect, waking at noon to make a cheese sandwich, reading Vicki's old blog entries for hours, and trying to sleep and not do laundry, until I had to work again.

I'd been making drinks during this rumination and I had to dump an entire shaker of Redheaded Sluts because they tasted like candied wallpaper. I mean, more than they should have.

Francis said, "Sam. I can't stand it when you're in pain."

"We're going to find her. Tonight. I'll make it worth your while."

"Outside of my just-stated needs, nothing is worth my while, Sam. Certainly not Vicki."

I said, "I'm not talking about Vicki. I'm talking about me and Vicki. That's a different moral imperative, one that involves loyalty and self-sacrifice."

"On my part."

"Yes. That's the pitch. You can erase years of emotional debt in one night. I will also buy. Not to mention that anyplace Vicki will be, there's sure to be attractive girls."

Francis considered this. He ran his hand through his hair, again, think *My Own Private Idaho*, and then did it again in case any girls at the bar missed it the first time. "You make good points. I would argue, though, that this will put me one ahead. You will owe me. I will be able to do something unspeakable in the near future and you will have to back me up."

"I always have."

"Reasonable people can disagree, but okay. I'm your wingman for getting back the girl who, with three short months of sucking your terrible dick more than a year ago, caused a lifetime of pain."

"Francis . . ."

"Okay. Sorry. I'm in. How do we find her?"

"I don't know. Let me think. No, that's a bad idea. You figure it out while I work."

Francis would think of something. It would be something that would satisfy his needs first, but, eventually, I'd get what I wanted. I had always trusted him to get me into and out of whatever trouble was needed—ever since the first time when we were kids running from the cops, the 40s of Ballantine in our backpacks shattering or tossed aside, all but the two Francis kept his fists on, over fences and suburban New Jersey hedgerow. A tornado or hurricane or wrath of a prohibitionist god could hit and I'd lose all my bottles in fright and clumsiness but Francis would arise unscathed, with enough beer for us to stay drunk for an afternoon at least.

Virgil dipped out to get a slice before I left for the night. I served customers, cleaned glasses, and restocked beer, all while thinking of Vicki, the way she used to drink. The way she'd wear thrift-shop flannel in the summer over expensive shorts, with her skin playing peekaboo from all directions. How she'd never bother to push her hair back when she tilted back a bottle of Jim Beam she'd stolen from another bar and brought to whatever club she'd gotten us invited to. She'd lean back with the bottle and no one would stop her. Security guards would laugh; she was so tiny and the bottle would look so big up against her mouth.

Down the bar, Sarita was allowing herself to be pulled close to Drunk Fireman and then abruptly pulling away. Drunk Fireman looked like he was going to burst.

Francis told Sanita, "Sam and I are going to find Vicki. He's going to woo her."

"Oh good. I was hoping this year would bring more Vicki into our lives," Sanita said. "JK, Sam. You know I love that girl."

The skinheads were getting rowdy. They had pretty much taken over the corner by the *Addams Family* pinball. That didn't bode too well for the cracked glass or for Virgil's tips. Half a dozen thugs in flag-covered bomber jackets camped by the entrance of the bar wasn't exactly an invitation to the college ladies and yuppie men who rent-paying bartenders needed on a Saturday night.

Francis muttered, "The crew is getting cute. That'll end well for nobody."

The skins were demanding their pints faster and in a more singsong fashion. That was okay. It was when they got quiet and thin-eyed that I got nervous. Well, terrified. I also worried when they were quiet that some customer might mistake them for harmless or, worse, gay. We'd had to drag norms out and call them an ambulance from across the street more than once for them mistaking the pack of psychopaths for fashionable lads who might want to talk footie.

The other problem was that I'd have to pass them to leave. And by that point their number one, Flannery, might be here. Flannery did not like me.

Under the watchful gaze of Murray and Drunk Fireman, I brought the skinheads their pints and waited just long enough for it to be emasculating to get paid. It might actually be a little easier for Virgil. They were so prickly about the "racist skinhead" tag that they sometimes gave him more room to breathe. If they decided to stay, and didn't throw a boot party outside the bar, some poor schmuck was going to get a bottle to the face on the N line back to Astoria.

I sidled over to Murray. "You hanging out tonight?"

Murray nodded. That didn't necessarily mean much. Murray wasn't the bouncer and if a better offer, drugs or female, came around, he'd be gone. Or if he just got drunk and forgot. But it was something.

Virgil reappeared and began taking orders. I counted the money and told him that the soda gun was wonky and that some girl was going to come in for her phone she'd forgotten on Friday and to give Murray and Drunk Fireman some free drinks to keep his ass from being beaten if the skins got frisky.

"Not concerned, my friend, about those confused motherfuckers. All that skin-head stress is from you and yours holding onto the past. They're just jocks to me. I don't see them in my head before I get here and I don't see them in my dreams when I leave. Anyway, only the Puerto Rican ones will take a swing at me. The others want me to like 'em. Not going to happen but why advertise? In the big picture, these dudes don't exist. Anachronisms with no place to call their home. Fuck them all day long."

He poured us each a double Jameson. I found his zen calming. Virgil had been sliced with a box cutter by punks a few years back so his fatalism was subculture neutral.

Virgil raised his glass. "To ass. Good luck on your mission. Always liked that girl."

I clinked and drank. "She'll be mine by dawn. Noon tomorrow at latest."

Francis already had his coat on. I stuffed my tips in my front jeans pocket. San-ita and Sarita took cigarettes out of the chest pocket of my thin winter coat as I put on my layers. White thermal over band T-shirt. No scarf. My mom would be seriously bummed. Francis was dressed the same, like an idiot, but he had a hat and maybe the patches on his jacket provided some warmth. Thanks, Amebix. Thanks, Tragedy. Thanks, Motörhead.

Francis rolled his eyes, "Aaaaand . . . Flannery is here. Sam, you go first."

Flannery Bianchi—de facto leader of BQE Boot Brothers, one of the last real skin-head crews in NYC, interracially nationalist, broadly hateful, and specifically feral, and the only crew that was still more concerned with pummeling strangers than dealing drugs or forming bands—had hands that were a wonder. Larger than his wiry arms would imply. They were hard origami, almost Cubist in the irregularities of the flesh. A lifetime of construction, combined with a lifetime of connecting with flesh, plaster, bone, glass, gave his hands detailed scarring that went past the wrists. Past that, everything was obscured by truly terrible tattoo work that crept up to his neck where a cursive *Only God Can Judge* framed a face that was almost pretty, in a vague fuzzy way, like a stage idol viewed from the cheap seats. His gray eyes were looking at me, but I was staring at his outstretched hand.

"Sam. Hey. You don't shake?" Flannery's head was cocked like he found me a bit perplexing; like a hawk finds a mole.

I repeated the mantra in my head that I always did when getting vibed by Flannery. I had stolen his girlfriend. *Do. Not. Flinch.*

I took his hand but the instant the pressure grew I pulled away. Too fast. Damn. I had already lost face. Behind me, Francis was making a show of talking to a girl in a High on Fire hoodie, pretending he didn't see what was going on.

"We were on our way out, Flannery. Good to see you," I said.

"Cut the shit, Sam. Vicki's back. I know what you know. I. KNOW. What you fucking know. Fuck you thinking? Not for nothing, Sam. Not going to happen." He punctuated the *I know* with a two jabs to my chest with his index finger.

The skins behind him gripped their pint glasses. Drunk Fireman stood up. Murray felt around under the bar for his cane. Francis stopped talking.

My fist clenched and unclenched involuntarily.

Flannery looked at my fist and then back in the general direction of my face, and laughed. "Sam. Real talk. Do not PRESUME to be a man. You know?" He patted my face and I let him.

I pushed around him and Francis followed. The hoots of Flannery's crew followed us out. I had sucked my first cigarette of the day halfway down before I started to breath again.

1-8 AMSTERDAM 2000

EIGHT
SKINHEADS

SEVEN BARS
ONE NIGHTCLUB
ONE LOFT
& A DINER

"Where we going, Francis?"

We were walking fast down Second Avenue, both eager to pretend none of that had happened.

"I sent a few texts. I, for one, am definitely getting laid tonight. Girls love this romantic shit. You're juicing up the entire city for me."

"That's fine. I just want to find Vicki . . . before anyone else does."

I didn't doubt that Vicki could and would love me again, but what if a distraction got there first when she was in a blackout?

"Oh man. Old times. Flannery pissed off and us trying to find Vicki at a bar. I feel years younger!"

"You look it." Actually, he looked cold. We were both shivering.

Francis said, "Okay. First stop. Normally we'd check Pym's first, because if Vicki wanted to see you, that's where she'd go."

Francis saw my face.

"Sorry. Vicki DOES want to see you, but she doesn't know it yet. Where would she go whenever she got bored during your shifts . . . ?"

"Down the Street."

"And here we are. Pill better not charge us. I need money for drugs later."

We pushed hard on the door next to the unmarked black window that was down the street from Pym's but was also actually called "Down the Street." Or "DTS." Or, to its regulars, "The DTs." As habitual bar crawlers and tenders knew, it was easier sometimes to just refer to wherever one was going to as "the bar." "You going to the bar?" "Yeah." "Maybe see you later." And we always somehow knew what the other person was talking about. Maybe by the direction their nose twitched.

Some band that sounded like the Yeah Yeah Yeahs but wasn't was playing. Pill threw a rag over his left shoulder and bear-hugged us over the bar.

"My boys! I never see you!" Pill smiled at us like we were pie.

"Hey, Pill," I said.

"Hey, Pill," Francis said. "Just beer, please. Sam's got a thing."

"I heard Vicki is drinking again. That the thing? Or is it an Aviva thing? So many things, Sam. You heartbreaker."

"Funny, feels different than that. The former."

Pill had to put his hands in front of his face to figure the latter/former deal.

"Vicki! To dream the impossible dream. You know, we still have some of her photos in the back? Bet they're worth something now that she's big-time. So talented that one."

"Have you seen her?"

"I sure have! Last night, in fact. Here you go, boys."

Pill put a couple Brooklyn Lagers in front of Francis and myself. He pulled his round glasses off his perfect sphere of a head and wiped them and then his white forehead. His body was round too.

I put a twenty on the bar. Pill didn't touch it.

"You know, Sam, I always felt bad about what happened with you and Vicki. She is such a sweetheart."

Francis coughed.

"Oh, Francis. She is. Remember when she didn't have money for a cab and she got those sanitation workers to drop her off in their truck? God, when they started honking and we all ran outside and there she was, hanging outside the passenger window of that . . . that TANK. I just about died."

I remembered. We had fought in the bathroom for twenty minutes over the garbage guy giving her his number and it "only being polite" to take it, and then we'd fucked on the sink and then Pill bought us drinks all night long.

"I don't remember that," Francis said.

"Neither do I," I said.

Francis was reaching over the bar. "Pill, can I rub your belly? For luck? We have a treacherous night ahead of us. Need that Buddha luck."

"Fuck YOU, Francis." Pill let him rub his belly, though, rolling his eyes. In my experience no one turned down Francis.

"Thanks, Pill, if I meet you on the road, I'll never kill you."

Pill laughed, but the second Buddha reference seemed to sting a little. He walked over to two down-low black muscle guys a few seats away and felt their arms while they pretended to protest.

I picked at the bar, which was one of those steel jobbers with a glass-top inset. Under the glass were coins and pewter miniatures.

"Hey, Francis?"

"Yes, Sam?"

"You're with me on this, right?"

Francis looked into his beer and exhaled. "Sam, remember that time when we were seventeen and we took mushrooms and got thrown out of ABC No Rio during the Bugout Society show because you were pissing in the corner and then you shit your pants and I found you new pants and never told anyone?"

"Yes, except that it was *you* who pissed in the corner and it wasn't a corner, it was on an amp, and I shit myself because you had gotten us thrown out of the one place that would let two wasted teenagers use the bathroom, and you stole me leather shorts from the sex shop on Orchard Street and you told everyone, and you still bring it up every time I ask if you're going to help."

"Well, exactly. I helped you then and I'll help you now. I'm a very loyal dude. And you need not remind me of what you've done for me. Like an elephant, I am."

I'd paid Francis's rent in a New Brunswick basement for almost a full year until he was finally thrown out for having sex with every single person anyone in the punk house had ever dated, been related to, or met in any capacity whatsoever. Francis wasn't a predator but he wasn't great at remembering names or faces. My loyalty to him had cost me. But what could I do? We came up together, two fatherless creeps fumbling with the world's etiquette.

Francis reached over the bar and grabbed a pen and paper from near the credit card machine. He also violated basic bar etiquette by grabbing a handful of olives. At least these rules I knew. I slapped his hand.

Francis took no notice. "Okay, Vicki destination bars. This will be a good exercise. I think college told me something about this. Or maybe it was my dad's self-actualization courses. Before he actualized his escape."

Francis and I had almost identical dads in terms of guidance. If we didn't look so different, we could have supposed it was the same dad.

Francis made a graph. *Vicki* on the top, *plus Sam 4-evah* on the bottom. In the middle he started writing the names of Manhattan bars and lofts Vicki had spent time at in her hellion days. It was a long list.

"Cross off River Sticks and Remember the '90s, they both closed."

"Really?"

"Yep."

"Wasn't I 86'd from the '90s anyways?"

"Yeah, you kept trying to lure girls into the bathroom during CMJ, saying you wanted to 'sign them to your label.'"

"Gross. I hate CMJ."

"Doesn't bring out your best."

Francis said, "No. Anyway. Coachwhips, the Underground, Boiler Room, Tassles, the Package, Reverse Cowgirl?"

"Christ. Tonight is going to get ugly."

Francis motioned for two more beers. Synths and cool, cool vocals were in the air. Either She Wants Revenge or the Bravery were being played. Maybe it was the Faint but I was pretty sure I liked the Faint.

"Violence is inherent to the system."

I said, "Yeah, okay. Hopefully we can avoid the Underground. What about East Egg?"

"On a Saturday?" Francis looked at me like I was an idiot. "Impossible to get in. I mean, for us. Vicki got into all sorts of places."

"She and I got into those places. As a couple."

"Sorry. Untrue. She got in and you were with her."

There was a crash from the gallery in the back. It was normally closed on the weekends to keep weekend warriors from tagging up the art. Or throwing up on it.

An unlabeled back door flew open and the black-leather-jacket-and-no-shirt combo came running out, screaming, "WHORE!"

Francis and I swiveled our stools and said in unison, "Careful."

Stiv looked at us like we'd just crashed into his bedroom. What had appeared to be a heroin problem earlier appeared now to be general vacancy. His nose was bleeding and he leaned at an unnatural angle that failed to be rakish. Francis and I stood up. Stiv made for the street. He didn't look back.

Aviva appeared and struck an exaggerated karate pose.

"Hiiiiiiiii YA!" She faked a kick that brought her high-heeled boot uncomfortably close to my nose.

"Hi-ya, yourself, lady." Francis hugged her. Francis hugged a bit long for my liking. I pouted.

"Sam. You remember your wife."

"Hello, Aviva. You look nice." I may have been wrong about the necklace but I was sure I recognized the tights. I had loved buying Aviva tights. Every variety, from webbed to sheer to every pattern in every suit in a deck of cards, all the textures that could be rolled off the architecture of a woman's leg, and always black. These looked familiar. If she saw me looking she didn't let on.

Aviva did a low reenactment of her previous kick. "Sam. You prick."

Francis put out his arms to present her. "Doesn't she look amazing? Like *Sex in the City* never happened?"

"She does. What happened in there?" I motioned to the back room.

Aviva shot me a look and told Francis, "Stiv there thought brunch meant he could do what he pleased. It was just brunch."

"Wait . . . his name is actually Stiv?"

Aviva shrugged. "Anyway, what are you chumps up to?"

"Nothing," we said in unison.

All the fun drained from Aviva's face. "Oh. Okay. You know what? Fuck you both." In one motion, Aviva drank the rest of my beer and threw her faux fur on over the layered swathes of black. She grabbed her purse, saluted Pill, and was out the door.

Pill came over. "Oh yeah, I forgot. Aviva and some guy were here. I let them take a disco nap in the back cuz Aviva didn't want to go back to Williamsburg. She works SO hard. Did you know that when her boss provided the sculptures for that *Ant-Man* musical, every ant had to have its own 'energy'? Aviva had to design a karmic landscape for each and every one! And the pincers had to move so that it would be believable when they served as the Greek chorus! Boys, the art world is *crazy*."

I nodded. Francis was fiddling with his phone and suddenly barked, "We have a Vicki sighting!"

I started layering. A band that sounded like Interpol but wasn't was playing. Pill waved our twenty at us. Francis went to grab it but I swatted his arm down.

1 NEW YORK 2015
2 LOS ANGELES 2015
3 BAMAKO, MALI 2013
4 LOS ANGELES 2015
5-6 NEW YORK 2007
7 LOS ANGELES 2015
8 GOLD COAST, AUSTRALIA 2013
9 BELFORT, FRANCE 2009
10 LOS ANGELES 2012
11 AUSTIN 2015

ELEVEN
MOMENTS
ON THE
WAY TO
SOMEWHERE
ELSE

3

4

6

SEVEN BARS
ONE NIGHTCLUB
ONE LOFT
& A DINER

We were in a cab, Francis and me, crossing Houston, to a party where Vicki had been seen drinking chilled cucumber vodka. Francis was guiding the driver. I prided myself on only being friends with people who, regardless of their other faults, where polite to cabbies. You could tell a lot about a person, not just from how they treated drivers, but how they talked about them. I distrusted anyone who complained about how a cab smelled. And I treasured Francis for the way that he thought of cabbies as cousins to bartenders. He wasn't a fantastic tipper, but that was okay, I just always got out last and gave an extra dollar.

"Where exactly are we going?" I asked Francis again.

"Sea Building. Twelfth floor. I don't know if it's really the thirteenth or what. Do they still do that?"

The Sea Building. Jesus. I said, "Do what?"

"Not have thirteenth floors. Whatever. I'm not a building professor. It's the twelfth floor. Some party-promoter guy's place."

"You can live on the twelfth floor of the Sea Building on party-promoter money?"

"People love to party. But I imagine the money comes from somewhere else. From being awesome. It's Sebastian. You know Seb. Sebo."

"Don't we hate him? I thought he made his money in up-skirt DVDs."

Francis laughed. "That's just something I made up. I wish. No, I think he's just from LA or college or some shit. Money."

"And Vicki is there? I feel sick." My anxiety was pitching as we approached the tower.

"Don't feel sick yet. We're just getting started. She's there. My sources are immaculate."

"That's not what you mean, but cool."

The Sea Building was the most noticeable of the recent imbecilities plopped in the Lower East Side. Fifteen floors, plus penthouse, of aqua glass Lego, filled to the tippy top with, in their bland hubris and slim pretty functionality, the enemies of god. I supposed. It's not like I knew these animals. Its slogan was *See Yourself in the Sea* and its design was supposed to reflect "the oceanic diversity of the neighborhood."

The doorman eyed us, but we were white riffraff, and that was hardly riffraff at all. We nodded like we lived there and rushed into the elevator.

There were at least twenty pairs of disembodied shoes forming a row and turning a corner before you even got to the apartment door. I thought I recognized a pair as Vicki's. There were at least three pairs of chunky-heeled Mary Janes. Did she still wear those? And if she was wearing the sort of dress that went with heels, would she even go to a party that required their removal? There were endless girls' sneakers, the kind that deejays and models wore when they "didn't care about fashion." Vicki's views on the topic had always been situation specific. Which were her shoes? What were her feet like now? I had to ask her, to have those scentless and velvety feet dragged across my face.

We were met at the door by a sprite. A wisp of a man with thin blond hair that hands had run through to the point of heat evaporation, and glasses held together by wire and gossamer. I felt fat looking at him. I wanted to pick him up by the turtleneck and toss him somewhere. Not because he was terrible, but because he looked like he deserved to fly. He was held down by a tiny gray dog in his arms. The dog was one of those miniature aristocratic types. The only small dog I knew by name was a Chihuahua and it wasn't one of those. It was the other kind of small dog.

Sebastian sized us up to choose an appropriate greeting. "What is UP, mother-fuckers!" he shouted.

I was a little hurt that he didn't greet us in French. That he'd tamped down the fey meant he thought we were dumb. But Francis gripped his shoulders in camaraderie and Sebastian beamed at him. I maintained eye contact with the dog, but honestly broke first.

Francis said, "Seb. Point me in the direction of the fridge? I have some imaginary beer for it."

Over my genteel host's shoulder, I could see a number of men in mujahideen scarves. I felt sympathetic. We were pretty high up in these mountains. My breath was thin. I scanned the room for Vicki's . . . whatever magical haircut Vicki would now be making work in ways others failed monstrously at.

Sebastian's smile dropped for a millisecond. "Oh-ho. You are a funny fucking guy! Francis, right? Now I remember you two! You're Sam. Vicki used to see you, yes? We were *just* talking about you! And she used to say how *nice* you were! It's just so hard to find a nice guy, am I right? I'm a huge fan of you, personally."

I shook his hand and let him kiss both my cheeks and then moved past him. Francis handed me a martini glass. He was uncorking a bottle of vodka with an expression of glee.

Francis held the bottle up to the light, watching the cucumber slices sink and rise. He said, marveling, "Vodka that doesn't taste like vodka but isn't entirely emasculating."

I shook my head. "He and Vicki were talking about me? What does that mean? I don't like that guy."

Francis was unconcerned. "Guys like Sebastian don't exist for you to like them. They exist for you to be employed by them, and steal from them, and take their women. But only temporarily. In my experience, the women go back to them. Paying your own rent sucks."

I pointed at Francis as I held up the glass for him to fill. "I imagine paying *your* rent sucks too."

Francis smiled. "Yeah, sure. There's that. Bitches are fickle, am I right? That's why I work. Can't depend on anyone."

"Where's Vicki, did you see her?"

"Be cool. We can't barge in there without drinks. I want to drink as much free stuff as I can before we have to go to another bar and not get charged. It's the principle."

The apartment was spacious, the separation between kitchen and living room delineated only by a marble countertop and a real-estate agent's will. The walls were eggshell. There were bookshelves, but they were practically empty, with the few books mainly art books stacked vertically largest to smallest. It was exactly like I thought apartments like this would be, so maybe I was filling in the blanks. There were plenty of black couches that didn't look cozy. Everyone was standing. Everyone except those above Seb in the nightlife hierarchy was barefoot. One guy had on dirty sneakers and a T-shirt around his neck like a bandit's bandanna, so he must have been somebody's boss or drug dealer or pet graffiti artist. Francis hovered in the no-man's-land between kitchen and great white open. I wondered where Vicki was. I wondered where all the pillows were.

Another small gray dog, like a tombstone for a baby, sniffed Francis.

"At least the dogs are cute."

"I don't trust it."

"You don't trust the dogs?"

Francis scowled. "I don't trust other guys and their affection for dogs. Seems exaggerated to make them more human. And I sure as shit don't trust guys who compliment a woman's dog. That's fucking suspect. It insults everyone's intelligence. Especially the dog's. Anyway. Let's not overthink this."

A woman in a sheer black dress who wasn't quite a model reached for the cucumber vodka in Francis's hand, assuming he would release it. She looked surprised when there was resistance, though the smile never left Francis's face. She cocked her head to the side, lips parted slightly, increasing the pheromones being shot in his direction. I hated knee-jerk pretty-girl hatred, but Francis had his issues.

I nudged him. "Francis . . ."

"Oh. Sorry. Here you go, girl. Didn't see you."

She gave him a look that communicated disbelief and stalked off.

"That's cute, Francis. Passive-aggressive girl baiting."

"Fuck you. I like cucumber vodka."

"The distinction is noted. Where the hell is Vicki? This place gives me the heebie-jeebies."

"You're a Class-A worry wart. If you didn't have heebie-jeebies, you'd have no jeebies at all."

Francis started moving through the room. I followed. He touched the furniture, looked down shirts, made fun of belt buckles. Vicki wasn't anywhere. I didn't even see anyone who knew Vicki, at least not when I knew Vicki.

"Sam, come here and look at this. It's amazing."

Francis had his head pressed against a full wall window. He was peering down with an expression of unbridled joy. I felt a pang of jealousy. Francis, greedy as a sweet infant every second of his life, with a carnality that bordered on innocence, was once again finding some flickering light to distract him and sate that moment's desire.

"You said Vicki was here."

"Look at this. *Just look.* Thirteen floors up, I bet the rent is, like, a lot, and check out this view. I almost feel sorry for the guy."

Directly below was the McDonald's on Essex, the car park next door. If there was a moon it wasn't showing.

"Maybe he never looks down. I wouldn't."

"That's because you're scared of heights, not because you deny your own shitty view."

Francis and I both had our heads pressed against the window. Our host drifted up behind us.

Seb said, "You know, I am just SO dumb. You *came here* looking for Vicki, didn't you?"

"No. Just heard it was a good party. I'm real sorry to crash."

"It's all good! I like to mix it up! You are both totally welcome. I just may pat you down when you leave . . . I'm kidding, brothers!"

It looked like he would have very much liked to have been kidding. He refilled our glasses from a shaker in his delicate, multiringed hand.

"Stay as long as you like and *please* don't hesitate to ask for anything."

He moved on to a couple of girls who looked over his shoulder at Francis and me and laughed at something he said. I placed my forehead back against the window.

"He seems nice."

"Yeah, terrific, he has multiple copies of *Infinite Jest* on display."

"Where?"

"Look. One on that bookshelf and another on that table. By the *Artforum*."

"Do you think he's read it?"

"Fuck no."

I put the *Infinite Jest* from the shelf in my jacket, while Francis eyed a black-and-white nude photo hanging on the wall, individual track lighting for what looked to me like an American Apparel ad. Francis took my glass from me and drained it.

"Shall we?"

"We haven't even talked to anyone, we have to find out where Vicki went."

"Oh that. Sara Seventeen is working at Ironweed. She said Vicki is there."

"You got a text?"

"In the elevator." Francis shrugged. "Sorry! I've never been in the Sea Building.

And we got a book! If this night stays this boring, it'll come in handy. Rest our heads on it."

We toddled toward the apartment door as fast as we could. The room was crowded.

We were at the door when Seb appeared again like he was made of wind. I couldn't stand behind Francis without looking comical. I shifted the book, as subtly as I could, to my left, above the waist, and held it like I was trying to staunch a wound.

"Are you leaving? Already?"

"We had a wonderful time," Francis said. "I love your apartment. It's exactly how I imagine heaven."

Seb leaned in and we each accepted kisses to both cheeks. He wasn't even gay or European. He just promoted parties.

"You know . . . it's interesting, you showing up here. It's very interesting. I mean, I *always* loved Vicki. She always made the most *interesting* choices, good or bad. Even when she was just a kid, showing up just to steal, like kids do, she was just so charming, what she chose to take. And you could tell, just by looking at her, that she was going to be so much more. And now she is! She is just so beautiful, now. You know, I don't think that *Vice* or whatever could even *do* a cover without her now? You know? *I just can't envision that happening!* She told me that there's even a billboard on Houston coming. Coco in some jeans for god knows what, as if it matters. God, I hope I can see it from here. Even if I can't, I'll feel like I can. The way cool travels. That's what Vicki's eye *just does*. You must be so proud to have been with her." He looked at me like I was part of the catering staff and my break was over.

Francis was quiet. He would have knocked this smartly dressed delicacy out if I had nodded. But instead I smiled. I wasn't hiding the book anymore. I raised it to his face.

"Francis and I are borrowing this."

"Take it. I have two."

We picked up our shoes and, since putting them on would look like bowing, walked in our socks to the elevator. The walls seemed even cleaner than on our way in. I would have given anything for a Sharpie.

Francis said, "My favorite part was when you threatened the tiny man with *Infinite Jest*."

"I think I won that party." I tried to smile. I don't think it showed.

Francis pulled a beer from inside his jacket and, as the elevator door opened, drank it down.

When the elevator arrived at the lobby, the doorman was standing there with his palm up to receive the stolen book. I put it in his hand without a word. Francis placed the empty bottle on top of the book and, taking me by the back of my shoulders, marched me out the door.

1 LOS ANGELES 2013
2 SAN DIEGO 2016
3 NASHVILLE 2011
4 NEW YORK 2008
5 NEW YORK 2011
6 HO CHI MINH CITY 2016
7 BROOKLYN 1999

FOUR DOGS
TWO CATS
& ONE GOAT

3

4

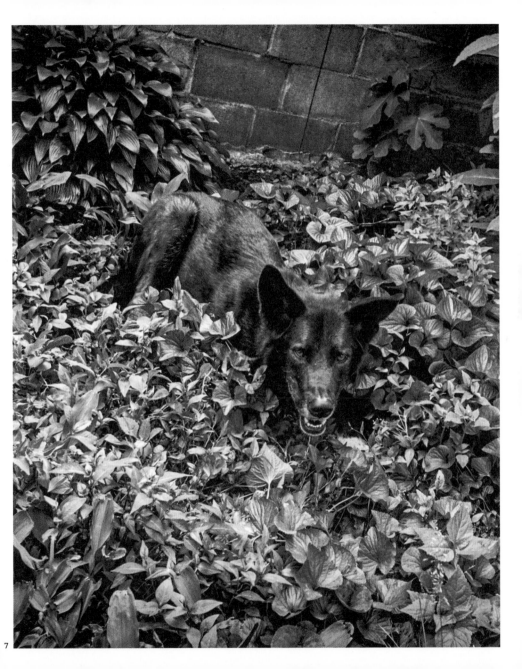

SEVEN BARS
ONE NIGHTCLUB
ONE LOFT
& A DINER

Before I moved out of the apartment I shared with Aviva in still vaguely industrial Williamsburg, when Vicki and I were deciding to stop just sleeping together wasted and try to have a relationship, I already had a lot of stuff in Vicki's Manhattan apartment. I rarely slept at my South Williamsburg apartment because my wife was there, with our "roommate" who I strongly suspected rarely slept in his own room. I wasn't in any position to judge, but I did.

My stuff started out, as these accumulations do, as a T-shirt Vicki borrowed so that she could sleep in it after we fucked. That became a T-shirt and a pair of pants that I spilled something on, or she bled on, so I had to leave them there. I'd borrowed some pants that had been lying around in the back of one of her drawers. I assumed they were previously Flannery's, but it wouldn't have been polite to ask. So the original pants stayed, with the original shirt, and eventually they were joined by jackets and more shirts: Supertouch, Sheer Terror, a few Fred Perrys. I may have usurped a few of Flannery's Fred Perrys too. The way I saw it, Flannery's loss was so huge and my gain so enormous that any attrition of clothing was the least of his problems and the least of my joy. And we were the same size, at the time. He'd since grown.

Anyway, single socks became pairs of socks that became shoes that became everything that I valued enough to not leave alone at my own apartment with my wife, the "roommate," and my wife's righteous and tactile rage. My wife wasn't averse to the cliché of throwing a cheating spouse's shit out the window. That's what the window was for. My wife and I lived above a bar where was a lot of foot traffic. I still see guys walking around in band T-shirts that I'm positive were once mine. In this way the redistribution of wealth is achieved, and in this way my wardrobe and comic book collection and my body and self became residents of Vicki's apartment, which, as luck would have it, was also situated above a bar. Since Vicki never complained, I assumed that my moving in was what she wanted. Living with Aviva had been hard, a constant negotiation of space and needs. We cried a lot even when things were great. She'd push me to explain things I only said as jokes, or she'd make me watch a documentary on Marc Rothko when I wanted to see *River's Edge* again. She'd ask how many pictures I'd taken that day. When was I going to switch to digital? Living with Vicki was easier. Vicki and I never cried and when we watched movies, she'd pick and then I'd watch her watch them. I'd laugh when she laughed, which was often. And Vicki didn't bother me about how many pictures I took. She was busy taking her own.

Living above a bar was pretty common in the circles we (me, Francis, Aviva, Vicki, etc.) ran in. It's cheaper to live above a bar and there are a lot of bars. We (me, Aviva, Vicki, etc.) were not the sort of people who complained about the noise. Instead, as our neighborhoods descended into yuppified tedium, the bars below complained about *us;* our disrupting of trivia nights, poetry slams, and speed-dating happy hours with our slamming of furniture, exaggerated coitus, and clothes raining down from the second-story window.

Vicki (and then Vicki and I), however, lived above a bar we liked, Odell's, and it liked us back. We were happy to have a place where we could drink cheap and slowly at, before I had to go to work and she had to go out drinking, which was also work, both in who she had to glad-hand and in how she, at the time, drank. The owner of Odell's was happy to have two lovebirds in the window, playing pool at four in the afternoon. He let Vicki hang her photos on the wall and they let me brag about how I was the one who put the nails in.

Odell's was owned by an elderly black Korean man who didn't allow swearing but turned a blind eye to the gaggle of coke dealers by the bathroom doors. Odell's, being on 3rd and C, was one of the last spots where a dive bar could eke out an existence into the mid-aughts. Then Vicki and I weren't living together and, for unrelated reasons, Odell went to Florida.

Odell's became the Ironweed, still a dive bar by 2006 East Village standards; meaning by décor alone, with six-dollar Budweiser and nine-dollar Jameson. The crowd was older skinheads turned drug dealers, and thirtysomething hardcore guys who'd done some time but were now doing okay. It was basically a cop bar, but with no cops. Just the sons of cops and firemen gone to seed.

The culture of aging New York City skinheads is a hard one to wrap one's head around and most people don't try. For former New Jersey punks such as me and Francis, it was important to parse the delicate social webbing. And serving and drinking with these mooks required a certain amount of connoisseurship. Bascially: in the eighties god created hardcore and CBGBs matinee shows. He also invented drug dealing as a way to escape either the endemic poverty of the ghetto or the drudgery of lower-middle-class outer-borough shitheelery. There was a lot of overlap of hip-hop and white guys in Adidas tracksuits that I never quite understood, but the gist was that what had started as teenage youth crews evolved into actual white (with a sprinkling of Puerto Rican and black) ganghood. Without all the usual racist skinhead connotations but plenty of the violence. As these guys aged, the gang aspects diminished, but the brotherhoods remained. Francis, having played bass in plenty of minor Jersey tough-guy hardcore bands, was free and easy with these guys, but I—maybe because I always sided with the girlfriends in disputes; or maybe, as it was once pointed out by a gakked-out bruiser, just because of my "pussy eyes"—was still seen as a wimp. And that was from the guys who didn't even like Flannery. Flannery's crew straight up hated me. Especially his number two, Big Timmy. If I'd been invisible before Vicki, I was now communism, AIDS, and whatever make and model killed Ian Stewart afterward.

Having Big Timmy hate you was scarier than having Flannery hate you. Big Timmy did terrible things to large men and still wasn't 86'd from anywhere. I couldn't think of a greater testament to his legend. I'd seen him walk up to bouncers who just the week before had to drag him out of a place, five on one. He'd shake their hands like, *Well, you know how it goes, god didn't invent emergency rooms not for nothing.* And they'd let him back on in. What else could they do? I'd watch the bouncers shrug helplessly at their managers. *You want him out?* their look said. *You do it.*

The Ironweed, besides sitting in the place of such fraught Vicki-and-Sam history, was also where Francis's number one ex-girlfriend, Vicki's on-again-off-again best friend, Sara Seventeen worked. Sara got her name from when she worked at the American Apparel on Houston, where, along with a store culture that seemed to run entirely on MDMA and the possession of fake IDs rendered irrelevant by the serial dating of older Lower East Side bar staff, there were two other Saras. Usually, if you forget a girl's name, safe bets are Sara(h) or Kate. One Sara was seventeen, one was eighteen, and one, the American Apparel elder, was nineteen. Like so many New York nicknames, the names stuck even though Sara Seventeen was now twenty-three.

Vicki had been Sara's best friend since they were teenagers and just beginning to get older Queens punks and construction workers to buy them wine and tequila. When Sara was twenty, she and Francis had a torrid affair, or what would be considered by most an affair. For Francis and Sara Seventeen, a week was a long-term relationship.

The Ironweed was two long rooms, both with stained wood–paneled walls that could almost be called brindle. They were graffiti free. Tagging was a serious no-no. Even if the clientele had no shortage of former taggers, that shit was for other people's clubhouses. The first room, where the serving bar was, had the requisite deejay booth, where you could harass the deejay for not playing vinyl or, if he/she was, jump up and down to make the needle skip. There were a couple mirrors, strategically placed out of punching range behind the deejay booth and the bar. The back room still had a pool table, for fights and quarter stealing. Dimly lit booths surrounded the table, and beyond the booths there was the long line to the bathroom.

The moment we shoved our way through the crowd to get to the bar, the Upsetters' "Drugs and Poison" was blaring from ceiling-mounted speakers. There was a smattering of women in Trash and Vaudeville punk and rockabilly dresses, but Vicki had been phasing out the Stop Staring! look even when we first hooked up. Yet I was still a breathless wreck with every small-boned baby-doll dress that moved within my periphery.

Sara had a smile that was warm and wry. "Francis! You look terrible. You said you were coming by, but I assumed you were lying. As you do."

"Sara, you look beautiful. Like our sex tape come to life."

"I taped over our sex tape. Critics found my acting unconvincing."

"Then they never heard you say, *I love you*."

Francis leaned over the bar and gave Sara a kiss. She brushed her black hair from the side of her neck to accept it. Francis lingered. Sara looked at me.

"Hi, Sam. Looking for Vicki? I think she's still here, but honestly, I've been fucking slammed." She held up a finger of warning to Francis and he kept whatever joke he had in the offing to himself. She continued, "She may be in the back. She never says bye when she leaves."

The bar was two people deep to get drinks. The barback looked harried. The crowd was 70 percent men, with the females mainly sitting on laps or firmly protected in circles of glowering, tattooed strongmen. On these guys, tattoos still looked like warnings. Francis and I had shared history with most of these men. Respect was given to those who had been serving drinks through the rapid changes to the neighborhood.

Some, the ones who liked wiseasses and didn't take free drinks for granted, even liked us. These guys would smile, giving their pals permission to nod. We shook hands with everyone, made hard eye contact, showed respect. Francis, like I said, was more comfortable, but even he knew that booze mixed with limited female presence mixed with our way of talking—which could easily be taken, correctly or not, as condescension—might result in serious bodily harm. I could never remember how long I was supposed to maintain eye contact, so I looked at my drink a lot.

Francis and I worked our way to the back. I didn't see Vicki anywhere but I didn't really see much. Even though smoking had been outlawed in bars three years ago, after midnight the back room would fill with cigarette smoke. Along with the lighting, it was difficult to place faces until they were within kissing distance. Once upon a time that had been appealing. In a different crowd, Francis would be leaning in on everyone, taking cigarettes out of mouths to take a quick puff before placing them back into lips. But here he kept his hands to himself. He got engrossed in conversation with a baldhead in a dark-blue Fred Perry. Vicki wasn't here. I slouched into the bathroom line. I stared into my beer and waited to piss. I was feeling queasy but no way in hell was I going to do more than that in those bathrooms.

Peeing allowed me to consider the future. Exiting the bathroom, still anxious, I repeated various phrases I'd say to Vicki when I found her, what she'd say back to me, what I'd say back with a crooked smile, working that charm to remind her of what I knew she was missing. It was a ten-second reverie coupled with my staring at the fractal crack of my flip-phone. I could get nothing from the device and willing it to ring from that future was not working.

Then I got hit. The dumb vacancy got smacked right off me, a large open hand knocking the color from my face, replacing it with a new color.

I dropped my phone and my beer. Both shattered. I put my hand to my face. It was shoved into me by another slap. Flannery was really strong and had momentum heading into the men's room as I was coming out. Having smacked me twice, he didn't even bother to move. He didn't have to. Nobody breaks up a slap fight. And no one knows how to respond to one either. I sure didn't. My fists clenched, but if I threw a punch, he was going to seriously fuck me up. I'd been hit enough that I could control my instinct to tear up, but it hurt, and I was feeling the embarrassment more than the pain. Everyone around us was. Some tough guys, who didn't run with crews as big as Flannery's, looked at me and then looked down.

Francis appeared by my side, and stood there looking warily at Flannery, who was grinning like a little boy who just learned to spit.

"I just fucking slapped your bitch, Francis. Like the fucking bitch he is. What do you think? You interested in doing something about it? Hit me with your purse?"

"I'm good."

"You're good? You're fucking good? You sure? I mean, there's two of you and only one of me so, if you aren't sure that you're good, fucking say something while I'm here, man to man, and don't back down like a pussy and make fucking jokes when I leave. I know what a funny fucking guy you are, *Francis*."

"I'm good. So is Sam. We're both good. Just looking for someone."

"I know who you're fucking looking for, why do you think I fucking smacked this faggot? That, and he isn't worth me closing my fist, I mean. I don't close my fists for queers. That's fucking prejudiced."

I was too humiliated to come up with anything to say, and for some reason I held out my hand. He gave my hand a look one would give something weak and diseased.

"Francis, I think maybe it would be for the best if you took your queer little buddy out of here. And I don't mean queer in the faggot sense, but in the I'm-going-to-fuck-ing-end-his-piece-of-shit-pussy-life sense. He fooled Vicki, but he never fooled me. You can't fool me. I *am* truth."

An interesting observation. I had to agree. He felt like a very true thing when he hit your face with his hand. People too often forget what truth is until the Flannerys of the world remind them.

My face was bleeding. Francis walked me to the front of the bar and people parted like they didn't want to catch what I had.

The deejay put on "Somebody's Gonna Get Their Head Kicked in Tonight." When we got to the bar, Sara Seventeen said, "If it's any consolation, Sam, he couldn't pro-tect me for shit either."

I was relieved that her contempt for Francis trumped all.

Francis looked hurt. "Fuck you, Sara! It was open hand!"

We pushed our way out onto the street. Francis lit a cigarette for me. When I took a drag my gums stung. All of a sudden I wanted to hit everything.

A group of youths passed by and I hated the gloss of their hair, the cut of their jeans, their young, high, happy voices. The airbrush job on the back of one their leather jackets, a neon hodgepodge of Nic Cage crucified on a cross, surrounded by angels, pushed me over the edge.

"What does your jacket mean?! It's just dumb! I hope everyone at NYU gets fuck- ing cancer and you die!"

My spittle landed near their shoes. They didn't look impressed.

Francis put his hand up. "Sorry. He just lost a fight. Keep walking. *You* fuckers I can take."

The boys allowed themselves to be pulled down the block by their girlfriends in gold hoop earrings and streetwear. They were still giving us the finger and calling us old as they turned the corner.

I turned on Francis. "Fuck you, dude! Fuck you! What happened in there? What just fucking happened? I hate you!"

"Sam, I swear, if he ever hits you with a closed fist . . ."

"That's not a real thing, Francis! I mean . . . it is! But! I would have stuck up for you."

"First of all, Sam, maybe you would have. Second of all, I'm really sorry. Live to fight another day, my friend. And the main thing is finding Vicki, yes? Yes?" Francis looked at me with eyes that had crashed a million pairs of panties.

Who was I to blow against the wind? I knew I was mostly mad at myself. I spun around a couple times, something I'd done since I was a child so I could be dizzy instead of upset. I needed the old breath to be gone, so something new and cold could replace it. I was grateful for the winter air.

Sara Seventeen ran out of the bar. "Sam, I almost forgot. When you see Vicki, can you give her this? She left it behind." Sara wrapped a long red-and-white soccer hooligan scarf around my neck. She kissed me on the cheek. I almost asked about my phone, but what was the point? It was dead and gone. Useless, like me. Two peas in a pod, my phone and I.

Sara ignored Francis's outstretched arms and went back inside.

1 SAN LUIS OBISPO 2016
2 BROOKLYN 2001
3 LOS ANGELES 2015
4 BROOKLYN 1997
5 BERLIN 2003
6 LOS ANGELES 2014
7 NEW YORK 2010
8 AMSTERDAM 2013

EIGHT
WOMEN
IN THEIR
APARTMENTS

2

3

4

5

SEVEN BARS
ONE NIGHTCLUB
ONE LOFT
& A DINER

We went around the corner to 9th and C. There was a tourist S&M-themed bistro there and Vicki was friends with some of the doms. The doorway was an elaborate renaissance-fair pastiche: dragons, mead, whips, and witches in thigh-highs. I gripped the iron bar door handle with both hands. The door gave a satisfying *whoosh* as it opened against the cold. Francis followed closely behind. I asked him how I looked. He rolled his eyes but fixed my hair.

The bar was packed. Tables full of men in suits and women in red and black dresses pointing and cackling. The entertainment was the waitstaff and the slaves chained by ribbon and leather to the waitresses. The waitresses were uniform fetish models in red pleather. The slaves were paunchy men exposing enough skin to laugh at but not so much that a tourist would be put off their escargot and old-fashioneds.

On the walls were velvet tapestries with light pornography of the vaguely Asian variety. Kimonos and chi-fueled erections. In between awnings were more men, faces to the wall, entirely still.

Francis and I got our eye rolls out of our systems by the entrance and made our way to the back, where Francis's bouncer friend was working. Daryl greeted us with midlevel-complicated handshakes and half hugs.

"Francis, you got my text about Vicki. Always happy to be of service. Welcome to hell, gentlemen."

"Is that what you guys have to say or are you just talking about, you know, work?"

"Pick your poison, Big F. Hey, Sam, how you doing? You look like you got slapped." He pushed the *you* so it was a play homosexual/homophobic put-on. Bouncers. So confusing.

"Hey, Daryl. Naw, it's the wind. Bracing. Thanks for hitting us up about Vicki. Buy you a drink?"

"No thanks, Sammy. Two years sober this week. Feel great and check this shit." He grabbed my hand and made me feel his stomach.

"Damn, Daryl."

"Damn STRAIGHT." Daryl flexed a bit more. "But lemme hook you ladies up. Yo! Lady Charon!"

A waitress in a too-tight bustier strutted over, groveling man in tow. "I'm slammed. What's up?"

The slave sniffed at her shoulder and she slapped him hard.

"Hey, Becky, sorry. Two Jamies and a soda water for myself. That okay with you?"

He didn't sound like he cared whether it was okay with her or not.

She grunted and left. I scanned the room. I didn't see Vicki but there were back rooms.

"So you saw the girl?" Francis asked.

"Oh yeah, came in and did a couple shots. Gave me a hug too. Sam, no disrespect, but that girl feels good up on a man. Never should have let that go. Not to mention she's really come up in the world. Her credit card was *nice*. Not that we took it. I said, *Girl, your money is no good here*. Sam, I'm telling you. You fucked up."

He didn't mean harm. I said, "Yeah, trying to fix that. Hard to maintain a relationship in the bar industry when the lady no longer drinks."

"Vicki quit drinking? I was wondering why I hadn't seen her in like a minute! Girl could drink. Looks like it didn't take."

"She was in AA too. You never saw her? Or are you just being anonymous?"

Lady Charon came back. She took our tips. Her hand lingered on Francis's but not on mine. Then she turned and screamed at one of the men at the wall: "WHY IS YOUR NOSE NOT TOUCHING THE WALL, WORM? WHY?"

The table nearest the slave started clapping.

"I never seen her at a meeting. But, you know, there are a lot of meetings. I've seen so many church basements it's like I found the Lord. So me not seeing her? Don't mean a thing." Before I could ask if Vicki had told him where she'd go next, Daryl said, "Excuse me, gentlemen."

One of the customers had taken the show too much to heart and thrown a handful of stirring straws at the chastised wall slave. Daryl loomed over the yuppie to give him his first warning. The women and other men at the table tittered. A surprise humiliation, on someone they knew, how exciting.

Francis disappeared; scanning the room, I found him at the waitress station, leaning in on Becky. I suspected he was using Vicki as an excuse to show some interest. Francis could multitask.

I was troubled. Not being seen at the better-populated Alcoholics Anonymous meetings wasn't the same as cheating, but it felt similar. She'd started going to meetings when we were still together, leaving me reeling in an empty apartment over a bar we'd loved, with no one to drink with but my friends, who I hated. Had she been lying? Was she never going to meetings at all? Was Daryl lying? How strict could "anonymous" be? Did he have other reasons? He seemed real familiar with how attractive Vicki was.

Francis was suddenly next to me and handed me a shot. It was more lime juice than vodka.

I shout-whispered in Francis's ear, "Do you see Daryl and Vicki together? Like, biblically?"

Francis jerked his ear from the vicinity of my mouth and looked at me like I'd been insane for a while and he was tired of humoring me.

"Sam, that's insane. Or, whatever, if we're going down that road, then yes, sure, definitely."

"Don't mock me. You know how AA is. They all fuck and lie all the time. It's part of the deal."

"No, Sam, they all fuck and tell the truth way too much. And Daryl has no reason to lie to you. He's huge." Francis shook his head again. "I'm your boy, but come on, dude. Let's get out of here before your weirdness makes things at the S&M tourist trap weird."

Francis left a ten on the bar and we bullied our way to the exit. We were blocked by Daryl, who was throwing out the yuppie, gently but firmly. Yuppie's date was behind them, hopping up and down and trying to hit Daryl on the head with her shoe. Francis grabbed her shoe and threw it to the side of the room, where it beaned a slave in his head.

"Oh shit! Sorry, uh, worm! Thanks for your help, Daryl!" Francis elbowed me hard so I'd thank Daryl too, but I wouldn't do it. I felt jealous of Daryl's alcoholism.

But weather behind us gave way to the weather in front and we were out on the street.

1 LOS ANGELES 2015
2–3 LOS ANGELES 2016
4–10 HO CHI MINH CITY 2016
11–13 LOS ANGELES 2016
14 NEW YORK 2009
15 NEW YORK 2011
16 CLEVELAND 2015

FIFTEEN
WOMEN
WORKING
AT NIGHT

4-7

8-10

15

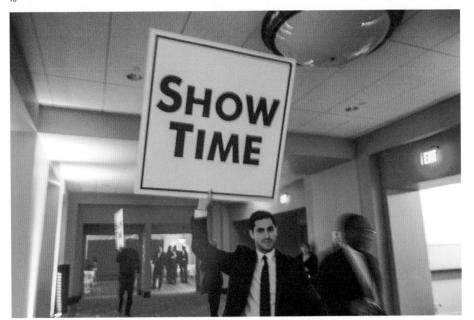

SEVEN BARS
ONE NIGHTCLUB
ONE LOFT
& A DINER

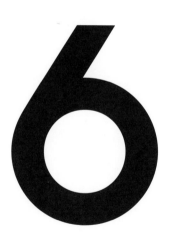

I popped my collar against the winter wind and wished I didn't look so good. A nice snowsuit with panda mittens, maybe a butt flap, would have been grand. It was insanely cold. We waved at a couple cabs but Saturday was catching up to us and none were empty.

Not having a better idea, and the FDR being one direction and the no-man's-land above 14th Street being another, we walked west to Avenue B. We saw Steve and Young Steve smoking cigarettes across the street so we ducked into a bodega to avoid them.

The bodega was shockingly well lit. Maybe I was drunker than I thought. The man behind the counter was most likely from Yemen and I almost greeted him with an "As-salāmuʿalaykum" but I never knew if I was being condescending or friendly or if I had the region/religion right, so I muttered a mishmash like I always did. I thought good intentions should telegraph themselves but Vicki had expected me, being eight years older, to know things. But I was always too afraid to offend to show off.

A couple Puerto Rican youths were standing up against the Little Debbie shelf. Their eyes were at half-lid, like they were extremely stoned or had seen enough videos to know what looked threatening. They were bobbing up and down as if to music. I didn't see any earbuds or hear any music besides the soft freestyle coming from the bodega radio. Teens and their unheard music made me nervous. I was scared of anyone, of any ethnicity, under the age of twenty. I avoided them and asked for the cheapest pack of smokes. Francis was oblivious and reached over one of the youth's shoulders. The sleepy-eyed kid jerked to the side.

"Ayo!"

"Sorry. Want a Cosmic Brownie."

"I got your cosmic brownie, faggot."

The other kid covered his mouth and doubled over laughing like his puffy vest was made of lead.

Francis backed away with his snack cake.

"Naw. This Cosmic Brownie. Little Debbie."

"You a little Debbie, bitch." He gripped his crotch and swayed toward us. We didn't budge and he stopped just in front of Francis. He was a few inches shorter and looking at Francis's chin. His Yankees cap pointed in the direction of the door.

I paid ten dollars for the generic cigarettes and ninety-nine cents for the Cosmic Brownies while Francis and Sleepy Not Sleepy looked at each other. I could see Francis weighing his options: can't hit a kid, scared to die, really want to hit the kid, scared to lose and look like a pussy in front of bodega worker, me, and God. I'd been through this a million times. I gripped Francis's shoulder.

"It's Saturday night. Cops everywhere and no one leaves the Tombs till Monday. Let's do this another time, hey?"

The kid responded in Francis's stead: "Yeah, yeah, another time. Or now. I don't give a fuck, grunge faggot motherfuckers."

Francis shrugged and laughed. "Fair enough."

We exited and lit cigarettes. The kids didn't follow.

"Wonder how many dudes those retards are gonna have to obstruct before they get the fight they want," I mused.

"I'll give it to them . . ." Francis turned around.

"Leave it. They're sixteen. You and I were the same way. Less fighty maybe. Just as retarded."

"Maybe you. I was awesome and polite. New Brunswick's sweetest."

I still liked to tease him about his very short-lived straight-edge past. "You wore an Earth Crisis hoodie and punched dudes for wearing suede."

"Ha-ha. Nailed to the X, Sam. Let's go find drugs."

"Vicki."

"Oh yeah. Love. Let's see what the magic eight ball says." Francis touched his phone. I huddled closer for warmth. "Castle Takes the King is having an open bar in back. That's as likely as not?"

Despite the fact that hardly anyone we knew paid for drinks, an open bar always instilled a quickening of the pulse. Even on the borderlands of 14th Street, what we jokingly referred to as "Uptown." Really It was Midtown we all feared: money and real jobs and bad shoes. Manhattan, it could be argued, was all Midtown now.

"Vicki did love an open bar. That guy from what-the-fuck still own Castle?"

Castle Takes the King was a rocker bar that, despite being horrifically out of fashion, had maintained a pricey location by Avenue A. It was near Stuytown and was financed by the singer of a New Jersey gothic-inclined pop punk band that had gotten enormous in the wake of Green Day. Francis and I pretended to never remember what they were called even though we'd worn their shirts in our tweens.

Cabs were still impossible so we double-timed to 14th and were actually sweating when we got there. There was a crowd of smokers in front of the place and a wait to get in while the burly doorman checked IDs with an electronic scanner.

Luckily, even though we didn't know the bouncer, we looked the type that rocker bars want on Saturday nights to offset the squares, so he let us cut the line. At most places, we'd be scumbags at worst and haphazardly dressed bros at best. But at a place like Castle, men and women with obscure patches were desired. A bar owner never knew who was taking pictures, and wouldn't want their Saturday nights represented by off-weight Midwestern girls in tiaras. We weren't as good as attractive women, but we'd do. A manager who vaguely recalled our faces ushered us to the bar and bought us shots.

"Thanks for dropping by, guys. It is INSANE in the back. In. Sane." The manager had shoulder-length red hair and a well-tended beard.

We were shoved up against a face-sucking couple. I searched the crowd, making small leaps to gain some clarity. Helpfully, Francis shouted, "Thanks for having us! Seems crazy up front too! Good for you guys! Hey! Have you seen Vicki?"

The manager raised his arms in an exaggerated fashion. His eyes were back on the door. It was his job. "No! Sorry! Madness!"

"Do you know who Vicki is?"

The manger shrugged and shook his head. "Mad! Ness! Go in the back! Patterson would LOVE to see you! Can't hang!!"

The manager thought we were someone else. Aging rockers all looked the same. We all have thin jackets and crow's feet around the eyes.

Francis winked at me and we followed the guy through the crowd. Closer to the VIP room, the hair got longer or more sculpted. The T-shirts became more threadbare. There were cowboy shirts. Tattoos meant to be asked about. It was like a retirement home for guys who had dated Suicide Girls. Mötley Crüe was blaring at a volume well beyond irony and beer was spilling everywhere.

Francis yelled into my ear: "I thought this was a rockabilly bar! This is hella unrootsy!"

"Saturday night! Concessions!"

At the curtain protecting the back room the manager pointed to us and gave the bouncer a thumbs-up. The bouncer, like the manager, was wearing a metal T-shirt from a band I didn't know. He waved us through.

It was an older crowd. I didn't see Vicki but there was a waitress I recognized. She must have texted Francis. She wasn't an ex, just on his to-do list. Next to her, Patterson Childs was holding court. When he laughed, everyone around him laughed. The waitress was extremely busy. She was passing orders to the bartender and making whatever drinks were within reach. New York licensing required a waitress for some establishments, so some bars sidestepped it by just having two bartenders, with one on each side of the bar.

Francis put an arm around the waitress and said something in her ear. She laughed and rolled her eyes. She was wearing a band T-shirt too: Lydia Lunch. Walking that fine line between obscurity and canon. I imagined that some of her pillow talk consisted of complaining about customers who thought she was wearing Joan Jett.

At the bar we were in danger of getting hit by Patterson Childs's expansive arm motions. I could smell his patchouli. He was wearing a three-piece black wool suit. His tie was also black. He had a wallet chain. His hair was peroxide blond and standing straight up. He had knuckle tattoos that he hadn't had in the nineties. His band was called Artemis Mine Artemis. Their shirt I wore as a baby punk showed the death of St. Sebastian but with a hot girl in the saint's place, pierced by arrows up to her bust. Patterson Childs might have half nodded at me, but he was so animated I couldn't tell for sure.

Francis was introducing me to the waitress though I didn't catch her name.

"I know Sam," she said. "Nice to see you again!"

I smiled too wide. She knew I was blanking. "Hi! Hey! Good to see you! . . . So! Is Vicki here?"

She yelled in my ear that some frat guy had spilled an entire beer down the back of Vicki's dress. So she poured a drink over his head and went home to change. My heart at once sank and vaguely soared. A near miss. I wanted so badly to see Vicki but I wanted her full attention when I did, not to be a bit player in her screwball antics. My organs raged against each other till my skin felt taut and damp. Apparently, the altercation had been hilarious. Apparently, Patterson Childs had found it particularly hilarious.

Francis ventured off to the bathroom so I held both our drinks. I was in the way of the waitress, with everyone trying to get drinks, and Patterson Childs's storytelling, but there was nowhere to go. The couches were taken and there were go-go dancers on every table. I stared at one's ass for a while. It stirred nothing but further anxiety. I remembered Vicki and I once being at another of Patterson's parties, another borderline-ironic hard rock night, where Patterson had extravagantly bought two shots at a time, even though the three of us were ostensibly talking. Vicki had whispered that I was being "silly" and unfriendly. Maybe I was.

The beer smell was now getting to me and I worried that when Vicki and I reunited, I would slur or tell an obvious lie. I felt heat rising. I was sweating.

Someone tapped my shoulder and I almost spilled my drink on Patterson Childs's beautifully pressed suit. He mock-jumped back and put his hands up. He laughed. Everyone around him laughed. Was I laughing? I was. But there was a sour tang coating my tongue.

"Dude! I know you! You work at Pym's Cup! Man, that place is wild!"

"That's right, man." We'd met over a dozen times.

"Man, I haven't been there is a minute! I did some dirt there, man. Holy shit! What's your name again? Sorry! I meet a lot of people!"

"Sam! I'm Sam!"

Patterson couldn't hear me.

"Never mind!" I shouted. "It's not important!"

"That's a crazy attitude! Every soul is important, motherfucker! I am SERIOUS! Every soul!"

If he'd finally heard it, he'd already forgotten my name.

"Listen! MY FRIEND! You dated that Vicki chick, right? She was just here! You missed her! Such a wild, wild lady! Fucking PSYCHED to see her out again, am I right?!

Man, when she called me last week and said she was looking to party, I fucking FLIPPED!" He leaned in close to me. "SUCH a cool, cool girl. You know? I saw her at a Fashion Week thing hanging with Mary-Kate the other night and she was looking fantastic. *That* was a solid hang."

What was I being told? Was it code? Patterson Childs's breath smelled of vagina. It mixed poorly with the patchouli. I thought about Patterson going down on someone, Vicki specifically.

"Excuse me." I threw up on Patterson Childs's suit.

He shoved me away hard, almost a punch.

Francis seemed to pull the pint glass out of my hand and drink it down while smooshing the face of our adolescent rock idol with his free hand all in one seamless motion. We were bum-rushed out of the back room. We tangled in the divider curtain and tumbled into the bouncer. Then it was all security and arms and we were being pushed to the front door, but there were so many people in the way Francis and I couldn't help ourselves. I grabbed at a drink and dropped it bottom-first onto a table, the beer shooting upward as the glass shattered. Francis grabbed a purse and threw it over heads toward the back of the room.

We landed hard on the sidewalk outside. It had started snowing, but that was barely a cushion. Francis and I lay there laughing. I hadn't gotten any vomit on myself. I felt light-headed and free of poison. The red-haired manager came out and yelled about "suit damages" and "cops," but then he got cold and went inside.

III

1 MONTREAL 2000
2 NEW YORK 1996
3 LOS ANGELES 2015
4 TOKYO 2012
5 MONTREAL 2000
6 SAN FRANCISCO 2000
7 NEW YORK 2012
8 LOS ANGELES 2015
9 MONTREAL 2000
10 BROOKLYN 2000
11 LAS VEGAS 1998

ELEVEN
GUYS

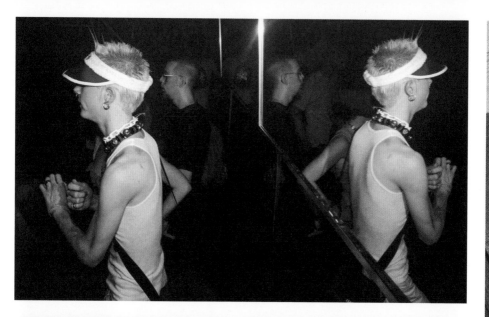

3

4

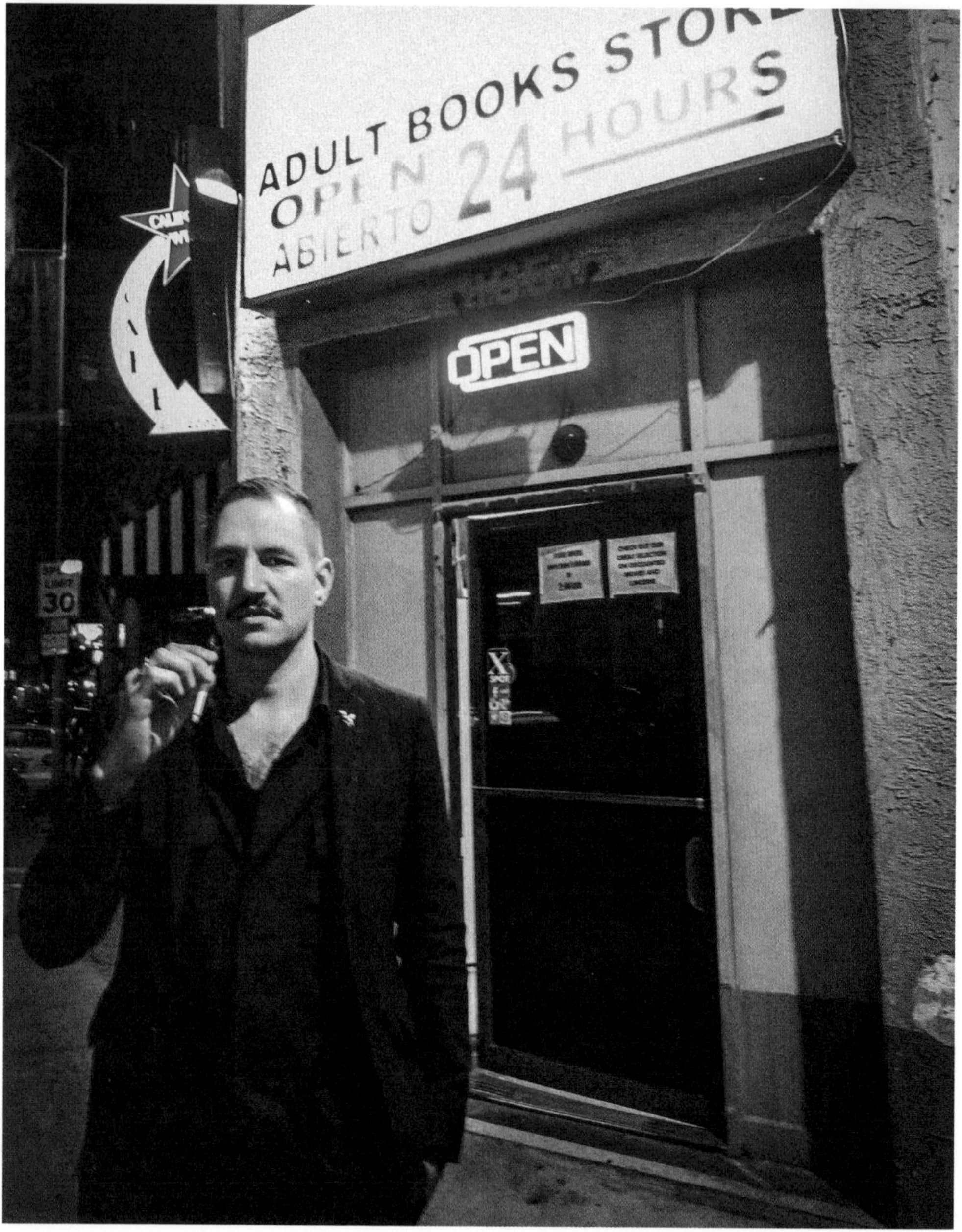
ADULT BOOKS STOR
OPEN 24 HOURS
ABIERTO
OPEN
30

9

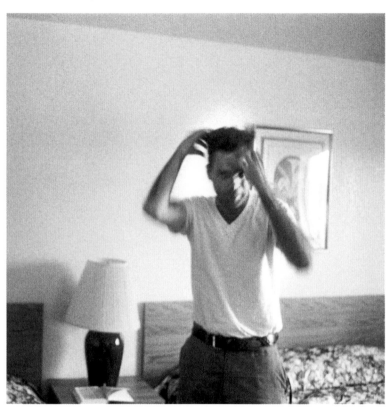

11

SEVEN BARS
ONE NIGHTCLUB
ONE LOFT
& A DINER

(AGAIN)

"You threw up on what's-his-name!"

"I know!"

"Ahahahahahah!"

"I know!"

Francis dried his tears of glee and said, "Let's go back to Pym's and regroup. How long will it take Vicki to get uptown and change?"

We knew Vicki was living above 14th now, some rent-subsidized place that was technically her godmother's. I knew she was very quick at changing clothes and she'd do her makeup in the train or cab. Maybe I'd always been rushing her. Reasonable people could disagree.

"That idiot wanted me to think he fucked Vicki."

"Huh. I didn't get that. But I trust your instincts. And the waitress wasn't interested in me, by the way. Topsy-turvy night."

I patted Francis on the back.

"Oh," he said. "I saw Aviva in the bathroom line. She says, *Fuck you, Sam*."

Everybody I'd ever cared for was truly taking it to the hoop tonight. Was it a full moon? I ran my hand through my hair and it came back wet. Beer and vodka and snow. I popped an Altoid.

When we got to Pym's Cup, we were silent from the cold. It was crowded with people we knew. If you live in a city, you kiss a lot of cheeks. What starts as mockery of Europeans and fashionistas becomes habit. Then cheek-kissing becomes a bit of a grab on the side. Just a little grab. It's not cheating. It's barely sexual. But some cheeks do get kissed for longer, sides get grabbed with a bit more hand, a lot of fingers. It's amazing how many people you can touch in one night. By the time Francis and I had made our way to the back, my face felt chafed and not from the cold. Before we even reached Sanita and Sarita, I had to pull Francis off a sort of regular, sort of ex–someone of his in a Black Flag T-shirt.

Virgil shook his head as I spun Francis up to the bar. "That girl is bad news. Looks like she's played every role in a cum-shot compilation."

"Naw, Virgil," Francis said, "she's cool."

"Didn't say she wasn't."

Neither Sanita nor Sarita laughed at the banter. Being women, they knew how quickly they could be put in the punch-line category. Vicki had never been down with this way of speaking either, but there was a sly faux-concerned cruelty sometimes to the way she'd talk about other women. Every girl Francis took to was "damaged" and "badly in need of realignment." She didn't call anyone a slut, just "sad."

We'd all known Vicki since she was a teenager dating Flannery. That was something we had all discussed at length, this sweet crazy girl going up and down with a horrifically unsweet skinhead. Then there was this night when Aviva was hungover and in one of her periodic boredoms with everyone we knew and stayed home and I went out with Francis and we'd gotten into it pretty hard. We stayed at the now-closed gay bar White Swallow until past closing and ended up at some indie film actress's sublet on 23rd Street, where nothing good could come of anything. There had been the usual assortment of types; graffiti artists, bass players, an ex-lover of Mapplethorpe who was paying for all the drugs. We pretended to be dismayed and full of scorn and Francis disappeared into an upstairs bathroom with an illegible-chest-pieced lady who he of course would end up friends with. By seven in the morning, it was down to myself and some Peter Pan Posse graf guys and Vicki. She was tired of screaming Nas lyrics along with Choko, one of the more prominent artists, and I offered to split a cab with her. Her shirt was torn in interesting ways but I thought I was being a gentleman.

Vicki had looked at me sideways and said, "Let's walk. Clear our heads."

My heart went evil and I agreed.

Vicki already had her place above Odell's but was watching some *Paper* magazine photo editor's apartment in Greenpoint. We went through half a pack of Parliament Lights on our way to the Williamsburg Bridge. Being a Sunday morning, traffic was sparse. The wind was a proper fall bracing and we alternated between huddling against it and parting when the morning sun hit our eyes and made us warm. We were coked out and laughing. We made fun of everyone we'd ever met. We never mentioned Flannery or Aviva. I talked about photography over her talking about photography but she didn't seem to mind. I talked about my dad or what I imagined was my dad. She told me she'd be famous for being great and not stupid and that self-actualization was a choice she'd made after considerable trauma. It felt like the realest thing anyone had ever said to me. I told her that there was nothing more important than friendship and that all I wanted to do until I died was take pictures of my friends and show the whole world just how amazing they were, to capture their spark. We looked at each other. A lot. Sharing deranged grins that got more subdued the farther we walked. My hand brushed hers approximately a thousand times and I told myself it was unintentional. When the daylight cut through the cold, we defied it, acting like every contact was just what drunks who didn't want to freeze to death did. Halfway across the bridge, she leaned into me and I pushed her away. Then I changed my mind. I kissed her hard against the fencing on the bike lanes. It was a short kiss because we were already out of breath. The second kiss was longer and I had a finger in her pussy, my wrist almost breaking against her jeans button, before I even saw a breast. I'd sucked my finger dry by the time I got home to my wife, who was cutting lines as I walked in. Aviva had been drinking tequila since I'd left and was mad at me and we fought the rest of the morning about every unkind thing either of us had ever said and passed out without fucking. In the afternoon, I woke up and silently jerked off while Aviva slept. I looked at her and thought of Vicki and came harder than I had in months. It was as close as I had ever gotten to a threesome.

"Sam. Shot. What are you doing?"

Virgil was looking at me like I was drooling on the pillow. There were seven shots of Jameson. Sanita, Sarita, Virgil, Francis, Murray, and Drunk Fireman all grabbed theirs. We clinked glasses haphazardly.

"Up with us. Down with them."

Proper shot etiquette: maintain eye contact. No one smiles until all glasses were slammed back on the bar.

Francis belched. "We need drugs."

I said, "We need pizza."

1 LOS ANGELES 2016
2 LOS ANGELES 2004
3 NEW YORK 1998
4 LAS VEGAS 2015
5 NEW YORK 2001
6 LOS ANGELES 2015

SIX
BATHROOMS
I WANTED
TO
REMEMBER

5

6

SEVEN BARS
ONE NIGHTCLUB
ONE LOFT
& A DINER

We set off to purchase drugs. We knew the Package always had a few guys working, but it was way over on Attorney Street, and the wind was a Wendigo at the throat of a Yeti, with our two skinny bodies caught between. Francis bumped into me on purpose for warmth.

    We hit a few places on the way: Boiler Room, Cherry Tavern, Loose Lips, Cheaters' Heaven, then Cherry Tavern again because Francis left his phone there. We did baby shots at every bar. The Blue Lounge, Up the North, Chat & Business. I was sobering up again from the walking, the seeing no one, the scoring of nothing. It was getting me down. It was like the daze I'd been in since Vicki walked out on me a year, two months, and a week ago. I hadn't even fucked anyone. I'd gotten coy a couple times and put my hand on a boob when it would be rude not to, but my heart, and correspondingly my cock, was never in it. My camera was either on my shelf or in my desk, I hadn't taken it out since I'd moved. I didn't see any sparks and if I had, I figured it was for someone else to capture. If I just got Vicki back, I knew I could attain flight. She'd always had notes around the apartment, stated goals like, *The world is what you make of it, so make it beautiful,* and, *Break the chains of "no."* I wanted to be caught in her headwinds and propelled forward with her. When we were together, we put our groceries and rent on her parents' credit card and spent my tip money on drinks and karaoke parties where I didn't sing. I broke my long-standing rule of *No flasks at the bar* (bartender's dictum: *Don't bring sand to the beach*) with Vicki because her job of mixing and mingling, now that *Paper* was giving her regular assignments, required so much time in bathrooms, not even doing drugs, just talking with promotors and photo editors under the unisex toilet lights. Aviva and I had spent long hours in bathrooms too, but always just the two of us, talking out the night's misunderstanding or slights. Aviva kept tight focus on our finances. If we were broke and couldn't tip on free drinks, we stayed home. Aviva didn't provide spiritual encouragement, just deadlines. For a while I'd liked that—Aviva respected me and had high expectations. But I always knew I would fail her, like my dad had failed my mom; I figured I'd been kinder than him by getting out when we were only married and there were no kids to fuck up.

    I needed to find Vicki. It was the only reasonable solution for everybody. We had no leads. I was getting panicky. I was hungry too. While Francis haggled with a homeless woman wearing a sweater that said, *There's more to me than what you see*

. . . *Respect me!* I ran into Ray's Famous and grabbed two slices. When I got out, I was pretty sure Francis still hadn't given her money, so I gave her my change and marched him along; he waved away the bite I offered.

Francis said, "I hate to confuse my body by mixing. Plus . . . I had Cosmic Brownies."

The Package unashamedly spelled out its name in neon, along with an image of two extremely large hands gripping an equally large box at crotch level.

The naming of a gay bar seemed simple on the surface. The gay bars on the west side had generic enough names. Even the Stonewall, deprived of context, could be Scottish or, hell, Confederate. If you were in the West Village and the bar wasn't full of college students, you could safely assume it was a gay bar, even if it was named The Elderly Straight. Uptown and Midtown—past Chelsea, obviously—there were no gay bars as far as I knew because up there gays stayed in their nice apartments playing piano. But in the East Village and LES, the names had to be as crass as possible: the Hole, White Swallow, the Cock, the Fat Cock, the Gaping Asshole. Gay bars with ambiguous names attracted too many yuppies and single women. The single women went to them ostensibly to avoid being hassled and the bros followed, presumably on some Tucker Max genetic memory of how to pull strange in the most obnoxious way. It was a vicious cycle that the short-shorts and leather crowd wanted no part of.

There was a beefy door guy but he knew us or guys who looked like us and let us pass. The sign on the door said, *Please Respect Our Neighbors. No Shrieking or Loud Groping. Thank You.* There was another sign below it, designating the Package as a drug-free bar. That raised our spirits. It meant the place was on the local precinct's radar, and that we'd have no problem getting Francis what he needed.

We punctured the pitch-black entry hallway and drew back a thick red curtain. The bar was half-full, but the puttering smoke machine made distances strange. You could see faces, but furniture was so foggy that drinks seemed to be floating on clouds, with hands coming in and out of the mist. There was a short bar that could fit one bartender comfortably, so there were, of course, two. They'd removed their shirts to make room. They were both chiseled and taut. The violence of their physiques clashed with the sweetness of their faces.

Aviva, my former wife, was dancing on the bar with a man dressed as a sailor.

Dancing is maybe the wrong word. It was more a rhythmic stomping of her black high heels, synchronized with a heavy-metal-thunder throwing-back-and-forth of hair. She'd always loved Depeche Mode and she'd always loved spilling drinks, so the combination of two of her interests didn't shock me. No one seemed perturbed. The boys appreciated a good time when they saw it. It wasn't a *Coyote Ugly* sexy dance, she was just doing her thing—in this case, atop a bar.

I cupped my hands and shouted above "Personal Jesus": "I consider it a personal favor that you're wearing panties!"

She gave me both fingers.

Francis yelled, "I don't! Aviva! Hey!"

She blew him a kiss.

What the fuck was that? I smacked Francis on the back of the head. He didn't seem to feel it.

Francis raised his hand to order drinks. I smacked that down too. We had a mission within our mission and I wanted to stay true to that. Francis rubbed his wrist and scowled, but he knew I was right. We had to maintain an even keel. It would do no one any good for us to end up in a bathroom discussing nineties hardcore bands at each other. It would be four a.m. in just a few hours.

Francis said. "Right, you see anyone?"

"I don't know anyone here."

"Maybe the dancing queen?"

"Which one?"

"Don't be a homophobe, Sam. It's confusing."

"We're not asking her. I don't want to get into a thing with her."

I gave him a look I'd been giving him for years, and he put a little more effort into not looking up her skirt.

I had to admit, she looked quite okay against the damask wallpaper. I didn't think about her dancing partner. He was just a man dancing with my former wife on the bar. It happened.

Francis came back from the bathroom and pointed, less subtly then I would have liked, at a man who was 6'6", crew cut, wearing a below-the-waist leather coat and baggy pants. "He told me my shirt was cool and called me *chief!*"

Francis was drunk. This was 101 stuff. A guy that large has to be a cop or a dealer. They'll both call you *chief*, big guys get away with that, but only narcs are friendly to strangers. There is the occasional friendly drug dealer. He will be selling you baby laxative and ground-up oregano.

"Francis, keep it together, I want to find Vicki. I can feel Aviva's eyes drilling holes into the back of my head."

"Well, first of all, nobody is looking at you at all. Nobody cares. And secondly, I'm working on it! I just thought you'd enjoy my keen sense of detection. I am a boy detective! A boyish defective!" Francis went up on his tiptoes. I couldn't tell if he was kidding. "And thirdly, Sam, enough about Vicki, that's all you ever talk about!"

"Fuck you, dude. I haven't mentioned Vicki in months! I've been so stoic because I didn't want to be a bum-out."

"But you *were* a bum-out. Your face is a telegram; it's the fucking Pony Express."

"Fuck you a million times! I didn't say shit. And now I need help and you're being fucked up and unhelpful."

"You're talking about her so much it's becoming a chore."

"Francis . . ."

"No, Sam. You've been boring the shit out of everyone with your unspoken complaining, even before this. You were talking about Vicki by *not* talking about her. You were talking about her by pouting whenever anyone else was having fun. You were talking about her by insisting that staff pay for drinks. You were talking about her by making us leave the bar by four thirty. WHAT THE FUCK IS THAT? It's been bumming everyone out. They were going to have an intervention. I told them not to!" Francis was poking me hard in the chest, and then he stopped. Something by the pinball machine had caught his eye. He grabbed my arm and shoved through the crowd.

There were two men there. One short and old, one tall and young. The old one was holding poppers up to the young one's nose. They looked familiar. I was pretty sure I'd carded the young one before.

They greeted Francis with wan smiles.

The young one was wearing a shirt that read, *Punks Throw Rocks at Cops*. He looked at me like I was wallpaper. "Hey, Francis," he said. "You look like shit." He motioned at me. "Your friend carded me once."

"Good thing you only come in when I'm working then, huh, Marlo? Sam, this is Marlo and Chicken Wing. If you carded Marlo, could you please apologize?"

"Of course. Great to meet you. Sorry. May I ask how old you are?"

Francis winced but Marlo smiled.

"You may! I'll be twenty-one in a year and a half! You did the right thing. Luckily, Francis did the better thing. Now we *all* win." He patted my cheek.

Chicken Wing tightened his grip on Marlo's waist.

"What do you need?" Marlo asked.

"What do you have?"

"Thirties, fifties, and one-twenties."

One-twenties were for girls and gays, and thirties were for actual babies.

"Fifty, please," Francis said.

My stomach began to lurch at the prospect of doing drugs. The stress and romance and whiskey were shaking the sheets. My stomach had always been a second stepdad. If I ever saw health insurance again, I needed to get checked out.

Chicken Wing and Marlo turned and walked away. Were we supposed to wait or follow? Why did dealers never say what they wanted you to do? Francis and I looked at each other; we followed.

Chicken Wing pulled back one of the heavy red curtains that lined the walls and revealed an unusually slender arched door. We followed them down a dark staircase. The room in the basement was just like every other bar office. Bright lights and posters and coffee cups told the story of accounting and business that the bohemian bar décor endeavored to hide. We could have been underneath the Ironweed or Down the Street or Castle. Pym's Cup didn't have an office. Their paperwork was probably done on an abacus in a field of poppies. The Package's office was lit with those environmentally safe bulbs that make everything look radioactive. There were posters for *Scream* movies on the walls, a weathered couch, and outdated computers. There were small sugar bowls of cocaine sitting in the center of an IKEA desk, surrounded by beer distributor paperwork.

Chicken Wing pushed his white-and-ironed hair from his eyes and started preparing a bag.

Marlo grabbed a bottle of Jameson out of a crate. He saw my nervous look. "It's okay! Chicken Wing is the manager! Chicken Wing, do you mind if I open this?"

Chicken Wing ignored him and cut four lines on the table. Marlo took a long pull and passed it to me. I took a medium pull and coughed into my hand. Francis took a longer pull and coughed upward into the air.

I put money on the table and Chicken Wing took it without counting. He handed me a small baggie. Not bad. About forty dollars' worth. I could live with that. I passed it to Francis. He put it in the small pocket on the right side of his jeans. It was a good investment. It would keep him happy and focused. Until he lost it or gave it to some girl or just thought he lost it only to find the pastey bag a month from now after he did the laundry.

Now was the hard part. Marlo had cut out four lines. Unless one was for Eliyahu, I was expected to participate. I really didn't want to. I was too on edge. But I didn't want to be rude. And I needed Francis firmly on my side, and I had just gotten a lecture about not being fun. So I did the line. I gagged hard. I caught the vomit in my mouth, but only until I reached the wastebasket.

Marlo and Chicken Wing seemed unconcerned. Marlo handed me a napkin. Francis finished my line and did one of his own.

Chicken Wing offered to cut me another. "Cleanse your palate?"

"No, no thanks. Sorry."

"No worries, honey. We're all friends here."

I thanked him and I meant it. I was light-headed. I needed air. Francis and I headed for the door. Marlo patted my cock as we squeezed past him and I tried not to cringe, partially at my own coke shrinkage. He mouthed, *No homo,* and laughed, and I joined him despite myself.

In the staircase, Aviva was coming down. I was stomach-coked, penis-weirded, and desperate for air. I pressed myself against the wall to let her pass. I thought I was trying to be polite. I was pretty fucked up, but not so much that I didn't notice the look on her face. Just like when she told me that it wasn't the cheating so much as how little value I'd placed on her time. That she hadn't wanted to like me but I'd used kindness as a Trojan horse to get past her defenses and then laid waste to everything. I just wanted to get away. I hurried upstairs.

It took Francis a minute to join me. When he came through the curtain, he gave me a squinty look. "That was weird."

"What?"

"I didn't know you were so repulsed by Aviva. She touched your arm and you recoiled. You physically freaked like the call was coming from within the house."

"What? I did?"

"She wanted to do lines with us."

"I can't do any more lines right now."

"Yeah, got that. But you don't have to be a jerk."

"Shit. Was she offended? Should I apologize? I'll go back."

"Too late. Come on. I'm high. Gotta walk."

Francis, newly focused, pushed me through the crowd, into the nighttime frost.

1 TOKYO 2016
2 LOS ANGELES 2016
3 INDIO, CA 2009
4–5 LONDON 2013
6–8 TOKYO 2016
9 NEWPORT, KY 2004
10 BRUSSELS 2008
11 NEW YORK 2011

ELEVEN PEOPLE DOING THEIR THING

4

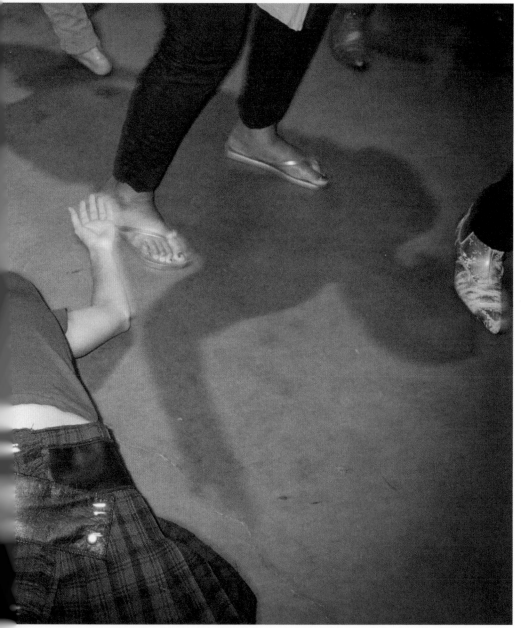

1 NEW YORK 2011
2 BROOKLYN 2013
3 NEW YORK 2013
4 BOGOTÁ 2013
5 NEW ORLEANS 2016
6 NEW YORK 2007
7 LOS ANGELES 2014

SEVEN
HAPPY
FEELINGS

2

4

6

7

SEVEN BARS
ONE NIGHTCLUB
ONE LOFT
& A DINER

8

Walking felt so good that I almost forgot about Aviva. It is not an easy world but it will occasionally hook a brother up: cigarettes, masturbation, what have you, the feeling you get when you're walking down the street and make eye contact with someone and just know, really know, that you could take them in a fair fight or have sex with them if you put in the effort. The small amount of coke was just enough to feel really, really good. Throwing up again was a fantastic idea too. All the drudgery was released from my hard-working tummy. I was less full of earth, I was an air sign.

Francis was high as fuck. His jaw was doing something unnatural. It was moving back and forth, playing doubles all by itself and, if not really winning, making a show of it. Francis's jaw was the opening credit to *The Patty Duke Show*. Cousinnnnsssss!

"Francis!" I shouted. I shoved him against a construction wall on Houston.

He swatted at me like I was a fly. "What?? Donbotherme."

I was already six feet away, leapfrogging over a sanitation can. I misjudged and tumbled over the second one. Francis laughed in hiccups. I didn't mind. I brushed that shit off. I kept brushing off my shoulder until Francis grabbed my hand. "Enough."

I unzipped my jacket, letting the soccer scarf Sara Seventeen had put around my neck give my chin moisture. Breathing and sweating were issues. It was snowing again. Francis dipped into a bodega and grabbed a bottle of water and we passed it back and forth, mumbling "Thank you" until that became a joke so that all were doing was passing the bottle back and forth, taking sips, and saying, "Thank you."

When it was gone Francis gave his face an extended up-and-down rub. "Okay. I feel better. I think I can drive. Give me the keys.'"

"Wait. Where are we going?"

"Fuck. Wait. My phone is confusing. Stop being confusing, I hate these things. You're not in charge here. Good guy, bad guy, I'm the guy with the phone. Ugh. Okay. Text thumbs . . . texting . . . Why are you so small, phone? . . . Texting . . . texted." Francis looked up like he'd solved a Rubik's Cube.

I felt a stirring of pride.

"Apparently, have to go to the Underground."

"Fuck."

He shrugged, looked at his phone again, shook it a little. "Yeah. That's what it says."

"FUCK."

"Yep."

We turned north. The Underground was on Avenue A. It was built upon the very lucrative economic principle that nobody gave a fuck. Not really. Not about aesthetics or charm or character or history. Cliché meaningless name? In a year, who would give a fuck? They'd just think of it as the name of the bar that they all went to. Banal wood finishing with the same exposed brick as every other date-rape emporium in the city? Whatever. Overpriced "specials" that consisted of one part vodka and one part Red Bull? Stop crying. Sluts gotta drink.

They threw a picture of Debbie Harry behind the bar and some Gnarls Barkley on the iPod and it was an "edgy" bar till the owners could flip it and open a theme club in the Meatpacking District. You could try to pry the quotation marks off the "edgy," but the bouncers would beat your ass first.

Then there was the staff. Everybody was facile-y good-looking and played bass in bands that too many nobodies had heard of. Their door guy was the worst. I hated him in a way that went beyond my not caring about him. His name was Blake Heathington. We all called him "Bland Hate-You-Something" behind his back. The last part would come. We fooled around with "Heifer-ton," but dude was fit. Too fit for my taste. Now that his electro-rock band was blowing up he only worked the door part-time. He toured Europe the rest of the time. Europe. God.

The eight short blocks were enough to wear down our buzzes to nubs of buzzes, wisps of happiness. Francis was still grinding his jaw a bit. That shit doesn't just go away. We were both rubbing our own arms and tucking our chins from the cold when we presented ourselves before Bland.

"Hey, Blake," I said.

"Hey, Bland," Francis said.

"Hey, Sam. Looking good, my man. Fuck you, Francis. Don't fucking call me that."

I said, "Sorry, Blake."

"Sorry, Bland," but Francis swallowed the last part into his chest. Then he looked up and smiled. I did the same.

"Whatever, you guys. It's good to see you, Sam. Really good." He gripped my shoulder like we'd served together. God, he was a prick. Handsome bores are the sneakiest people alive.

Francis and I slunk inside, glancing sideways at Bland, shrinking a bit.

I thought of the first thing I'd say to Vicki. I settled on *Hey*. The first thing one saw when one entered the Underground was the series of stripper poles. Three of them, equally spaced, on a semistage a couple feet off the floor. There were tables on either side to discourage too much high-flying stuntage and to give the bottle-service patrons something to talk about. There were no strippers for these poles. The poles were for female customers. Nothing says "bad time" like stripper poles without a monetarily compensated snatch attached.

Francis and I rolled our eyes in unison. Our fortitude was on the wane. We were snobs, sure, but what could we do? Francis started manipulating his house keys in his pocket. I jerked his hand out of his pocket. This was a bathroom-drugs-only kind of bar. I didn't see Vicki.

"Francis, if Vicki isn't here, I'll die. I may die either way."

Francis just said, "Yeah, yeah, me too."

The bartender was, to my mind, overdeterminedly hot. I liked to think I was disinclined toward *Penthouse* measurements and Japanese-lettering tattoos, but I felt a stirring between self-loathing and attraction anyway. Francis could read my mind and rolled his eyes again. He was losing patience with me. He handed me a twenty to get shots and went to powder his nose. I stood by the bar feeling conflicted. I didn't want to spend money there. Not even Francis's money. It was crowded and I kept getting jostled but I didn't want to lean on the bar and give the bartender the wrong idea. So I kept jerking away from it like it was electric. The bartender and her cleavage watched me like I was going to order a glass of water. I looked down her shirt for too long not to order something expensive.

"Two Patrón shots, please." I flashed a *V* for victory. She asked if I wanted them chilled and I cringed, humiliated. She put down limes and salt and I pushed them away to make the point to her cleavage that I was all man.

Francis came back, grabbed the salt, asked for a lime, and said, "Thank you, lady. You look fantastic."

The bartender smiled at him with her entire body and didn't give me my change.

I choked on the Patrón. Liquor so soon after vomiting and coke and pizza and anxiety will do that, but it was a ten-dollar shot so I got it down. Francis was already ordering more. I craned my neck to see past him, scanning for Vicki or even her imprint against the walls. I felt tears welling up but I beat those back too with an exaggerated pinch of my upper cartilage. The bartender thanked Francis for his tip a little closer than necessary.

"She seems nice," I said.

"She's awful. But I think I've been with all the good ones. At this rate, I may have to take her home in a year or two. I hope not. Just in case, I'm going to give her a reading list now."

"And maybe tell her to lose the exposed thong."

"Don't be a snob, Sam."

Francis was having his own nose issues. He grabbed a napkin from the bar and wiped himself. He put the crumpled napkin in his empty shot glass. I pulled him to the far wall before he could order another round.

We had momentum of all sorts, so we almost piled over a group of young professionals at one of the tables. The men looked up with a unified jerk, but seeing our eyes and the amount of sweat pouring out of us, they settled on whispering into their lady friends' ears about our limited prospects. The good thing about square joints with hep veneers is that if you have a little wear-and-tear and a bad coiffure, the regs will assume you're either famous or dangerous. Or that you're the barback.

We nestled up against the wall and surveyed the room.

"Who told you Vicki was here? All I see is date rape and bike lanes."

"Ha-ha. I have that site bookmarked. My boy Maxwell 57 was making a delivery and thought he saw Vicki coming in. I don't see her but I do see some girls I'd take into the bathroom and compliment their shoes."

There was a Joan Jett–looking cocktail waitress whose surliness seemed unaffected. There was a blown-up photo of Joan Jett behind her. It was almost Victorian. The net impression was like the Frick museum with Hard Rock Hotel wall hangings and uglier furniture. All the females had exposed shoulders and the men had their shirts tucked in.

"Maybe you can take the bartender to the bathroom."

"Don't be crass, Sam. You're being hostile because she's hot. That's why girls hate you."

"Wait, what? You were just vicious about her! I was just trying to fit in! Wait . . . girls hate me?"

He didn't answer. Then he got a startled look. I followed his gaze. I almost grabbed his arm.

Flannery was making his way across the floor with Big Timmy. Big Timmy, huge, terrifying, homophobic in that he considered everybody not a skinhead a faggot, and Flannery's best friend. The homoeroticism of skinhead culture in general, and his and Flannery's close friendship, had, to my knowledge, never been brought to his attention.

I was scared of Flannery because he hated me. And everybody was scared of Big Timmy. Big Timmy was bad enough that he could be called "Timmy" to his face. On him, it didn't seem cute.

"Never Tear Us Apart" was blaring from the speakers hanging from every ceiling corner. It's hard to feel satisfied with your life when "Never Tear Us Apart" is playing. I think it's the strings. I really, really didn't want to get beat up to INXS.

Francis said, "Love this song," and started pushing me toward the exit. "I forgot. I saw Flannery in the bathroom." He stopped to grab a drink from one of the table bro's hands and gulped it down hard.

"Francis. Fuck. I mean, really."

"Agreed. Walk faster."

The dude whose glass Francis had stolen got up, saw Flannery and Big Timmy moving toward us, and sat the fuck down. His girls didn't even give him shit.

We got to the door. Blake filled it and we had to slow down. It couldn't look like we were running. I wanted my body intact. I wanted my pride intact. I wanted Vicki intact to my body with a universe of blankets separating the two of us from Flannery and Big Timmy and Bland Heatherton . . . and even Francis and his skinhead-forgetting and bartender-charming and outbursts about how unpopular I was.

Blake didn't look like he felt like moving. The eighties hits kept coming. "Money

Changes Everything." I felt like the fat kid in *The Goonies*. I was sweating profusely and I felt like everyone was laughing at me.

"What's up, guys? You just got here."

I didn't think Blake was trying to be malicious. I would have liked him more. There was a *chief* hidden in his *guys* that I didn't think he even knew about.

Francis full-on body-checked Blake. I apologized as I slid past him.

The freezing air reminded me of why I was there.

"Oh, hey, Blake, by the way. Was Vicki by tonight? I need to . . . give her something." I hated saying even that much to him. I hated his band. They were going to make it.

"She was, actually." Blake looked sheepish. It made him look like a puppy with stupid hair.

"But, hey, Sam, that reminds me. I sort of have something I want to talk to you about."

I had a bad feeling. I dug my hands into my pockets.

"I know you guys broke up forever ago, so I hope you see things in a cool way. I don't fuck with a bro, if you know what I mean. I mean, right? You know me. We go back. I'm straight-up. And like I said, I think you're fucking rad. So I hope we're still cool. But listen, Vicki and I are sort of hanging out. I totally respect her, man."

My nausea returned. I had to take my hands out of my pockets. Tight jeans and fists are ridiculous.

"How long has this been happening, Bland?"

Bland took it. "Aw, Sam, c'mon, man. You guys are history. You should want her to be happy, dude. I know you really want her to be happy. You're a good guy!"

"Francis, am I a good guy?"

Francis looked over Blake's shoulders. He was shivering, like I was, but Blake didn't seem to feel the cold. Presumably from muscle, and the inner warmth that superior breeds have, like a warm, shiny coat on a show dog. Us mutts were born to resent the Clydesdales. My analogy was flawed and I wanted to shove it down the throat of the man who put that smug full-lipped mouth over Vicki's clit. I imagined a scene that I wasn't going to be able to stop imagining until I got much drunker or died.

Francis yelled, "HEY! FLANNERY!"

Flannery and Big Timmy were right behind Blake.

"HEY! FLANNERY! Guess what!" I called, pointing two triggered fingers at Blake. "Bland here is schtupping Vicki." Then I waved. "See ya!"

I was already running alongside Francis. I didn't care how it looked. I heard something hit something that sounded like ham on concrete. Running was within code as the ugliness that was about to happen was the kind that brought cops.

We stopped around the corner and I leaned into Francis. The freezing air burned my throat and I pulled Vicki's scarf over my mouth to breathe through. It smelled of beer and spittle and Altoids.

"What the fuck? Do you think Vicki would do that?"

Francis poured more of his coke onto the webbing between his index finger and thumb, brought it to his nostril. "Anybody will do anything. Always." He looked up at me seriously, wiped his face up and down from his hairline to his chin, paying extra attention to his eyes. "No, wait . . . *Every*body will do everything. ALWAYS."

He offered me the almost-empty baggie. I waved it away. When we were dating, I didn't mind the thought of Vicki fucking someone else. I acted jealous on occasion because I thought she'd look down on me if I didn't. But now that I wasn't there, the one she'd go home to, I was madly jealous. Jealous and wide awake to the infinite world of cocks that had been invisible or merely theoretical. Revelation was a feral bitch.

"I need to talk to Vicki, Francis. I *need* to talk to Vicki."

173

1 NEW YORK 2001
2 HONG KONG 2013
3 MARRAKECH 2011
4 HONG KONG 2013
5 NEW YORK 2013

FIVE
PLACES
I WENT
TO BE
ALONE

1

5

SEVEN BARS
ONE NIGHTCLUB
ONE LOFT
& A DINER

(AGAIN)

When Vicki walked out, after less than half a year of what I considered total bliss, it was the first time in my adult life I'd been dumped, and not just dumped but completely Batman'ed upon: no note, just a sharp "Goodbye, Sam" that I'd declined to believe; left the apartment for me to ride out the lease; erased me on MySpace and Facebook (which I'd *just* joined to make her happy). I soon realized that she wasn't even going to pick up the clothes that she'd left behind, so I made pillows of them, spread them over the bed like a child's stuffed animals. She told mutual friends that I was "emotionally unavailable" and, worse, "in sexual and spiritual stasis." So I started going to AA meetings. Well, actually, to coffee shops and bars *near* AA meetings. I didn't know what meetings she was going to, and I wasn't a stalker. I'd just hang out across the street from church basements, from the West Village to Williamsburg, drinking coffee, watching people with problems, people with problems who were actively looking for solutions. And I should mention, AA was like NA in the eighties; people were *good-looking*. I mean, from across the street. I saw some really attractive girls. And a lot of guys I used to know. They looked great too. Sobriety lent some of these dudes a wolfishness that they'd lacked when they were sloshing along Avenue A.

I also went to Film Forum by myself a lot. Really caught up with all the depressing things that had happened in Eastern Europe for the last forty years.

There were also days when Sanita and Sarita had to come to my apartment—our apartment—and throw me in the shower to get me to work on time. I was a wreck, but I ascribed it to everything else besides Vicki. I hollered about principle, about back rent, about Sanita and Sarita's failure to fully appreciate what I was going through. I may have even thrown out the fact that I'd left my wife for Vicki. Not sure what kind of sympathy I was hoping to gain there. Francis used to laugh into a half-full bottle of Maker's Mark when I got on that jag and change the channel. I had four channels. The cable was disconnected. The cable box was smashed. When I walked to the nearby Internet café, my e-mails were short. I only wrote to Vicki. None returned. She was gone from all social media, like a monk or zealot. I cried whenever Francis went out to get more cigarettes. I kept the apartment far longer than I could afford.

Then I stopped missing her. I mean, I thought I did. I should have taken it as a sign that I didn't even sleep around and then pull the classic "I'm not over my ex" as an excuse to not call. Done right, girls will even thank you for your honesty. But I bothered no ladies with my penis and lies. So I figured I was dully mature as far as that went. Hearing Vicki was back tonight made me miss her again as if the island of Manhattan was tipped and broken like the *Titanic*, and there I was, romantic and cold, really, really cold, standing on the top. I was sinking but it felt more exciting than life had been in months.

"Sam, I don't like you right now."

"What?" Francis was being very strange and not making fun of me. We were walking quickly west but he wasn't making jokes and, most worrying of all, he wasn't swerving.

"I'm the one who's supposed to be a jerk about girls. You're supposed to be nice or at least pretend to be nice."

"I am nice!"

"Well, for a guy who left his wife for a teenager, sure. For a guy who dropped all his friends when he was enraptured, sure. You talk a good game and it's one I value. I need a self-righteous friend because otherwise I'm sure to die by choking on someone else's vomit. I need you to be boring. And when Sara's mom died and you didn't say anything because you were too sad and then wouldn't go to the memorial Sara threw because you didn't want to run into Vicki—"

"I didn't want to make a scene! I was hurting."

"Yeah, okay, but, you know, one way to not make a scene and still be there for your friends is to, you know, just not make a fucking scene. And that's all fine. Really. Because you're the feelings guy in this partnership and I'm the bad boy and it's okay if I had to take a backseat when you were with Vicki and put up with a professional crybaby afterward. But then it's important that your PC front of feminist tut-tutting is maintained. If you're going to be rude to Aviva and shitty about big-boobed bartenders, which is my job, then I don't know. I just don't know what's happening."

Francis was red in the face. I hadn't seen him show so much emotion in years. It really got my attention. The first time Francis slept with a girl in our scene and then blew her off, we were in our teens. She was a little older and booked basement shows that Francis played. Francis was new to being in a popular band and new to how good-looking he could be. He didn't do anything terrible, strictly speaking, but she was hurt. She told people he was a shit, but, this being hardcore and the world, everyone sided with Francis. No one wanted to hear about it. But I was truly angry and I confronted him and made him apologize, for whatever that was worth.

Now Francis said I was violating the spirit of grand adventure, that romantic heroes weren't supposed to be small-dicked in spirit, that I had to step my game up, bring love to the hoop, stop being so garden-variety.

"You done?" I asked. He'd gotten to me, and he knew it. I'd fallen into habits I'd once despised. It was too much to apologize for. Luckily, apologies weren't really our thing.

"Yeah." He looked at his phone. We were almost back at Pym's, where Sara Seventeen had gone after her swing shift at Ironweed, and where, according to the twenty texts Francis had received, she was planning to drink every flavor of vodka and make out with Virgil until Francis came to collect her.

"Well. Rest assured that I've been judging you harshly all along too."

Francis sighed. "Perfect. Just be better than me. That's all I ask."

Pym's Cup was having a late-night lull. All the stools were taken but there was room to move. Virgil was playing with Sara Seventeen's hair and Sara looked like she might have been crying, but with the weather outside and the heat in the bar, so did most of the girls. Maybe they had been; people could be cruel.

Virgil slid us each a Jameson and a beer before moving down the bar. I moved with him to give Francis and Sara a little alone time.

"Virgil, I'll tip for Francis and myself. He hates you right now."

"Oh, that white nigga is stupid. I started touching on Sara when I saw you nerds coming. She's not my type. I won't fuck a girl who can't be buried in a Jewish cemetery. My mom would kill me."

"Right. My mistake. You keep a strict covenant."

"Well, it ain't exactly sacrosanct. But that's Francis's girl. I know that. Don't matter if she is currently not on his dick. She will be again, and forever, amen."

"Amen. Virgil, I can't find Vicki. I feel like I'm losing it."

We'd gotten down to Sanita and Sarita's end of the bar. At the sound of Vicki's name, they both emitted low moans, followed by a "Still!? Fuck!" in unison. Then they yelled, "Jinx! Buy me a Coke!" at each other and clinked glasses. I knew they were really on my side. They'd have frozen me out by now if they weren't. I was lucky to have such stalwarts in my corner. Drunk Fireman came out of one the bathrooms and patted me on the back too hard.

Virgil said, "Sam is getting existential about his MIA pussy. His heart is breaking. Let's do shots."

Sarita leaned into Drunk Fireman. Large as she was, he dwarfed her.

Sanita said, "Virgil, I can't believe you're still standing. Last round. Seriously this time." I could tell she'd been saying that for a while.

Virgil made a round of something weak and lemony. Customers were yelling at him, and even compounding cardinal rule violation 1,001 by waving money at him. I avoided eye contact so they didn't mistake me for someone on their team just because I was on their side of the bar. Want prompt service in this world? Know someone, idiot.

There was a crash of broken glass and we all looked. Francis was shouting. "I love you! I fucking love you!" at Sara Seventeen. He picked her up by the waist and put her on the bar, knocking over her drinks. Sara laughed and wrapped her legs around him. She bit his neck. The entire bar held its breath and watched Francis put his hand up her skirt.

"I haven't wiped the bar in hours," Virgil said.

We did our shots. Francis carried Sara to the bathroom and yelled over his shoulder, "Sam, I believe in love again! As soon as we're done in here, we'll go find Vicki! Watch the door!"

I put my scarf on the bar. I thought about Seb and Bland and Patterson. It was no great thrill to contemplate what they had and I didn't. Even Virgil got recognized on the street by skateboarding trainspotters. He got flown all over the country because people liked his fucking blog. He was someone. I had one picture in one skate book and I hadn't been paid for it and I was pretty sure I'd been included only out of a larger, more universal sense of pity that I could only hope to someday tap into again. I was a blogless moron, unlovable by reasonable standards. I hadn't wasted my potential. Potential had passed me by, preferring the company of other men.

When Sara and Francis emerged twenty minutes later, I had gotten thoroughly anxious again. The clock was ticking on my salvation. I at least needed to visualize and then actualize the kind of success that Francis and Sara Seventeen shared so audibly. I rushed into the bathroom after their exit and relieved myself while Francis held the door for me and shared a cigarette with Sara. At that point, what mattered? I came out and dried my hands on Francis's sleeve.

"Okay, Sam. Meatpacking District."

Sara grabbed me. Her just-fucked (or something akin to it) flush got to me. Bodies are wildly attractive when you know what they're capable of. I had to remind myself not to lean into her.

"I want Francis back in an hour," she said. "Bring him back to me or I'll cut your balls off." She reapplied my scarf and tightened it.

1–2 BROOKLYN 2000
3 BROOKLYN 1996
4 BROOKLYN 2001
5 NEW YORK 1996
6 NEW YORK 2004
7 BROOKLYN 1998

SEVEN SALAD DAYS

4

SEVEN BARS
ONE NIGHTCLUB
ONE LOFT
& A DINER

Waiting in line at East Egg sucked. I was stewing. Francis was stewing. Standing in line to get into a club is not something that lends itself to inspiring introspection. The soul is diminished and the company is irritating. It's easy enough to see why *they're* not getting in. And if one is honest with oneself, it's easy enough to see why the people getting in ahead are getting in ahead. They are more attractive, famous, or cool. You can tell yourself that the door guy is a fool, that money talks, and that if there was justice in the world, you'd be inside, being fellated by management. But if you can't stand the *system*, and the violence inherent to it, then you have no business going to a club. Stay home, play some nice house music, put the TV to static.

Or wait in line.

Francis somewhat subtly finished his coke. He and I were moving quickly through a new pack of Camel Lights. Quicker still thanks to the losers bumming cigarettes off of us. Some of them were attractive and, really, neither of us smoked anymore.

Francis mused, "There used to be white people in this town worth knowing."

"Excuse me?"

"Look, I'm as racist as the next guy, no doubt, but I know people *should* move to a city to ape the blacks and the gays. I'm for that. Electroclash didn't bother me. I got tipped in more pills and BJs than I knew what to do with. But this? All these Stephen Stills–looking motherfuckers with their V-necks that seem to go lower every year, talking like they're black? No thanks."

We were in a line of about forty people. Most of the men were white, facially scruffy, expensively hoofed. In the summer, old-man hats and V-neck T-shirts had been de rigueur for straight men who deejayed or graphic-designed. Even in the cold, some clubgoers were holding onto the look. Their gold hoop earring–wearing girlfriends pressed their pale skin up against the fur of the men's unzipped hoods. An Escalade drove by pumping Biggie and one of hippies started singing along. *"It was all a dream."* Then it was all of them, in unison. I knew all the words too. I felt so ashamed.

"And you KNOW these cocksuckers are banging out their girlfriends to white music. The whitest. Coldplay. Nobody means anything."

He discreetly fed himself a fresh bump, from a bag I didn't know he had. "Somebody needs to tear down the veil on these chumps. Their concerns are too varied."

"In the land of the dilettante, the dedicated hobbyist is king."

"Hodgepodgers to the last. The hodgepodge has many tricks and they all fucking suck."

"Agreed, but chill on that race shit. Seriously." I was glad his anger had moved from my failings to his usual foil of Hipsters Who Are Not Us, but I was also taking to faith his request that I go back to being a scold.

Francis rolled his eyes. "Grow up, Sam. I was making a point. And that shit isn't racist anymore. Black people told me."

"Anecdotal evidence can't set policy, dude."

"Whatever."

"Fine. Fuck it. Do what your racist ass wants. I don't care."

A girl behind us was describing a deli in her neighborhood as "totally ghetto." Francis gave her and her boyfriend a hostile stare. They didn't notice. They probably had their own bags of white powder in their pockets to insulate their worldview. There were veins of ice all over the sidewalk but nobody in the line was shivering.

I said, "Man, I can't believe Vicki would get with Bland, that fresh-faced goon. His cheekbones hate Jews. I didn't think I hated him as much as I hated Flannery, but maybe I do. Vicki has terrible taste."

"Present company excluded?"

"It's like, I like slutty girls. Sure. Girls know I like slutty girls. Girls know that I have the capacity to truly love and desire, even once marry, a slutty girl. So what does that do to a girl's self-esteem when I really love them? Sometimes being an asshole can just creep up on you." I took a drag on my cigarette. "I hope Bland didn't get killed."

Francis said, "That right there's your problem. In a fucking nutshell. Some dude loves your girl up and down, excuse me, and you hope he's not dead? Fuck that. Hope he's dead. I do. And I don't even care."

We'd been in line about twenty minutes. Neither Francis nor I were accustomed to waiting in lines. We knew people or we didn't go. All our friends were at bars where there were no lines and we were here. With no respite in sight. There were two door-men like there usually were, one white and one black. The yin and yang of the universe providing balance and order to Saturday night. The black man had his hand on the velvet rope. He was the muscle. The white man had a clipboard and a phone. He was the mouth of judgment. Together they were the godhead. They seemed miles away.

"There's something about a grown man with a clipboard that makes me want to kill," Francis said.

"That's why you're never getting into heaven."

"Fuck you. I am. You can be my plus-one."

We lit another cigarette.

If the Underground was avoided for its cheesiness or inauthenticity, then East Egg was avoided for the opposite. It got too many things right. It was only a year old and wasn't built with staying power in mind. It was a Futurist painting, grabbing every movement currently in vogue and throttling the juice out of it. The bartenders were mixologists and had Doc Holliday armbands. It was difficult to get a drink without ginger or something "muddled." The bathroom attendant was a former Tompkins Square Park bench character. I didn't like that he was in there shucking and jiving napkins and peanut M&Ms for a bunch of society-page interns whose claim to fame was that they'd blown Julian Schnabel's ski instructor in '02, been an extra on a Showtime series, or, more likely, were just born rich and running with it, from Vassar to publishing to marriage. Those were the women. The men were mostly deejays and party promoters.

"How do we know Vicki is here?"

When we dated, Vicki had had affection for all openings and the dumb things that came after. Already on the cusp, she was still shedding her street-punk skin so we both pretended it was all funny. We'd go to snicker at our betters, maybe hold up the bathroom line while we made out but rarely fucked on one of those new-style sinks, the kind that's flat marble with the water running over it. My jeans were usually wet and I was usually half hard and it was great. Eventually she did more mingling with our betters in those bathrooms. Then they were only *my* betters.

In Vicki's defense, my jeans were half soaked right up until she dumped me.

I'd assumed that she'd stopped going to bars altogether when she stopped drinking, but maybe East Egg counted as work. She'd gone from stark black-and-white photos of gutter punks, like mine but better, to glossy magazine work; she'd become Terry Richardson without the sexual assault. The transition required constant socializing, alternating with enough hibernation that she wouldn't be confused for a hanger-on. She'd gone from cutting down on drinking for early shoot calls to just being, well, gone. But if I could get inside the bar, I was sure a freshly drunked Vicki would be putting her panties in my hankie pocket in no time. Well, she had never done that. I was beginning to confuse the reasonable decadence of our shared past with a sexed-up fairy tale. Vicki needed me as much as I needed her. We were a team. I got her away from that jerk Flannery. I introduced her to people, was there handing out drugs and free drinks when she was schmoozing. I talked her through her work anxiety, taught her all the tricks I knew. I believed in her so much that I gave up my own photography when I compared our eyes and knew which of us understood sparks, or at least the world as it was. Yes, Vicki had treated me badly. But I would graciously buy her a drink and accept her apology. Or I'd apologize if that's what was needed. I knew sometimes that was just something men had to do.

"Sam, there's something I should probably tell you. And I don't want you to get weird about it."

I used my cigarette to light another and ground the original under my boot, handing the newly lit one to Francis, my friend.

"It's no big deal, but the reason I know Vicki is here is because Aviva told me." Francis was smiling with all his teeth. He flinched when I took the cigarette from his mouth.

"You've been texting Aviva? You told her we were looking for Vicki?"

"Well, should she not know? What exactly is the issue with that, Sam?"

"There's no issue! There's no fucking issue! Don't turn this around on me. You clearly see the problem or you wouldn't be sneaking around on your phone like some sort of phone asshole."

"Well, just because you get divorced from someone doesn't mean all of us get divorced from them. You can't have something as Antarctica for years and then one day decide it's just the North Pole. And I am your best friend. There's a lot of history there. And sure, I like Vicki; she says some funny shit and I don't begrudge her anything; certainly not making a mess of you. You did that all on your lonesome. And I don't begrudge Vicki snagging the one photo gig *Vice* offered you; you shouldn't have given it to her. No, Vicki saw her chances and took them. I respect it, even if I could have passed on all the new-age shit. Vicki is what's up and I guess we'll see how that goes . . . but your ex-wife is forever." Francis took a long drag. "So I keep in touch."

It was true that, when Vicki left, my friends all told me that she was a social climber and that she'd used my opportunities as her own, but really, weren't they *supposed* to say that? I mean, I wasn't going to take the *Vice* job anyway. I liked coke but not so much that I wanted it as my defining characteristic. I had friends who worked there, friends who maybe became better friends with Vicki while I was busy grooming my high horse. But Vicki and I were a team. Her victories were mine while I stayed pure. I put everything toward her career. Maybe Aviva had always pulled strings to let me use her friend's darkrooms, but Vicki had provided a more . . . spiritual heat. I needed her, clearly, or I was a loser, a bartender on the shore, watching cooler ships sail off to a cooler shore.

But I also didn't like being a character in Francis and Aviva's movie. In fact, I was suddenly feeling very angry. "That's impossibly dumb. *You're* impossibly dumb. You're a fucking traitor. A Manchurian candidate."

"Sam, you're being an immanchurian candidate. I didn't fuck her, just kept a respectful textful relationship. In case you ever change your mind. And, of course, to drive Sara Seventeen nuts."

"You were looking up Aviva's skirt at the Package!"

"Me and everyone else. She's a friend."

"Yes, but for everyone else it was purely clinical. Or double-checking their orientation. You were filing away fantasy footage. Or taping over previously filmed fantasy footage! You were expanding your film library of my wife's vagina! You prick."

"*Ex-wife* when it suits you, Sam."

This was throwing off my planned Vicki offensive. I was entirely disarmed and confused when we got to the front of the line.

"We're on Aviva's list. Francis plus one."

I was the tagalong? To get my girlfriend back I had to be my best friend's plus-one on my wife's list?

But it was cold, I was thirsty, I had to see Vicki at whatever cost. My ardor was real, even if the mark was now fuzzy and my eyes felt swollen. The clipboard glowed by the light of the phone. The moon was close. I followed the shade that was my friend inside. I felt as if an ending was coming up through my groin, past my sea-tossed tummy, up through my betrayed and betraying heart, up into my skull. It was pressing at my roof, trying to touch the moon. The tide carried me into East Egg.

Inside was another sea, stormy with air kisses. If Francis and I weren't such adept swimmers we would have drowned. And by *drowned* I mean we could have misinterpreted all that affectation for affection. I was all akimbo, an emotional muddle, and my metaphors were a fucking mess. We were embraced by people who hadn't seen us in eons, in donkey years, in *way* too long.

The walls were covered from floor to ceiling with curated street art. There was Neckface, Mike Giant, Space Invader. Hell, there was even some Shepard Fairey. Andre the Giant said *OBEY* from behind the bar, and enough time had passed so it was slick again. There was a large sign in the same font saying, *No Bottle Service*, as though East Egg's subversion of the megaclub norm was an act of moral courage on par with Shirley Chisholm's presidential bid. It was an act of pure contrariness. If it wouldn't clash so directly with the aesthetic of the place, they'd have charged $260 for a bottle of Sky poured in an Absolut bottle. And they'd have sold fifty a night. It was still twelve dollars for a tumbler of call.

I fished around in my pocket for twelve dollars.

Francis was kissing too long a girl who was looking over his shoulder at maybe nothing at all. And it was only three a.m. But those who are game find each other. I was having my cheeks molested by a large dark-skinned trans named Jackie, who I was actually glad to see. It felt good to hold a real friend. I had a strict no-snitching policy when it comes to those who prefer to keep their specific genitalia a surprise to customers I didn't know or care about. Jackie always appreciated it and she was one of the few beautiful types who still came by the bar after Vicki joined AA. I was finally within shouting distance of Vicki and my stomach was bouncing off my ribs in nervous anticipation.

Since it was three, the crowd's inhibitions were completely gone, along with any sense of their own speaking voices. I couldn't hear anybody because I heard everybody. Jackie was shouting and Francis was shouting. Some girl I probably knew, in an oversized New Kids on the Block T-shirt cut into a dress and tightened at the waist by crisscrossing belts, was shouting. I didn't bother saying real words. Francis put a drink in my one hand, took twelve dollars out of the other, and moved into the crowd. I'd see him again in an hour or a week. I drank. I rocked onto my toes and down again, trying to see over tall rockers' heads and through short girls' still-in-fashion Karen O hairdos. Hands were waving in the air like their owners just didn't care and I had to move some aside when they got too close to my eyes. Justice was playing at a deafening volume. Everybody was pulsating, mouthing the words or singing them. I was mouthing them too. *We. Are. Your. Friends.*

"Sam! Oh my god! What are you doing here?"

Vicki rose from a barstool and gave me the lightest of kisses on my cheek. Her shoes were black with just-outside-of-sensible heels. She was still wearing dark lipstick (that matched her nails), her eyes were still hazel, the mascara still seemed professionally applied, there was still a hint of blush on her cheeks but only just, and her hair was pulled back with the severity that libraries were burned to the ground in Greece just to dishevel . . . but there was something new about her face. She was smiling.

In a bar crowded past capacity, the stool next to her was empty. She patted it. I stood there motionless. Vicki patted the stool again.

"C'mon, Charlie Brown, kick the football."

I sat down and had to grip the stool with both hands. I said, trying to keep the tremor out of my voice, "I've been looking for you."

Vicki glanced over my shoulder and then gave me a distracted grin. "Cool! What's up?" The black-and-white vertical stripes of her dress under the club lights gave the appearance of movement, of a reel running out of a film projector.

This was not what I was expecting, to be greeted like an uncool younger cousin out on the town for the first time. "I miss you."

"Oh, I've missed you too! What have you been up to? I thought of you the other day when I went to get an egg cream and saw an issue of *Thrasher*! I can't believe that still exists! You should send them some your stuff."

I said, "I haven't been shooting much, to be honest."

Vicki raised both hands in mock horror. "Oh, but you must! It's so important to have a hobby! Oh, don't look at me that way. I'm sorry! I mean *a release*."

A man with a mustache, who might have been Terry Richardson, gave Vicki an affectionate arm grab as he passed. She waved and then gave me a look of *Okay, you have my full attention* that I gave to boring sad guys I served.

I said, "Vicki, I've been looking for you."

"Here I am!" She did a small wrist twirl with her drink. Martini glass. I hoped to god that it was a martini.

Was she talking like that because of the volume? Was she very drunk? I wanted her drunk, but I wasn't in the mood to be toyed with. Maybe I should touch her knee, move things along.

I moved in and said, "I didn't know where you went."

"I was in LA for a bit, did some yoga—Bikram, you know, the hot kind—had a bit of work there besides, did the bicoastal thing. Really, really great."

I involuntarily put my hand on my groin. "I brought your scarf."

Vicki motioned to the bartender for another drink. He smiled and didn't charge her.

"Keep it, lover. Or toss it. I'm telling you, Sam, letting go has brought me to the best place." Vicki pulled the red straw from her mouth and tapped me on the forehead with it. She was pretty drunk. "It's not good to hold on to the ephemeral. I stopped doing that and I feel so free. And frankly, my work reflects that. You should really try it. Release yourself from the parochial. Embrace the big city, sweetie. You'll thank me."

"Vicki, do you remember when we first met? You were with Flannery at Pym's Cup and you had a Chelsea cut that you were growing out and were wearing a tight Fred Perry shirt, black with a white collar, and a red skirt over ripped black stockings, and I saw you at the bar and I said to myself, *If I get that girl to look at me, it's all over.* And then you finally did, I mean really did, when we walked over the bridge? Do you remember?"

"Oh gosh . . . Flannery. That guy. I really thought he was the love of my life for a while there, you know? What a psycho. But sweet in his way. God, life is so funny." She took another sip from her martini glass.

"I left my wife for you." I didn't know why I said that. I flushed deeper.

"Well. Sam. I didn't ask you to do that."

"You didn't ask me not to."

"Aviva maybe needed a little push onto her path too. She always acted like she was better than me."

"I guess you showed her."

"Oh, Sam. People like you and Aviva love to wallow in drama. I bet it was exactly what you both wanted. A little disaster. I can't be blamed for my journey."

I could see the bathroom lines behind Vicki. Francis was in one line and my wife in another. They were talking. Aviva's layers were gone. There were visible straps of maybe a bustier. I thought I saw leopard print around a breast.

"What the hell does that even mean, Vicki? Your journey? Aviva was always kind to you!"

"She was always kind to one of us."

Francis and my wife were in the same line now.

"No. Don't make this about me. Don't be a bitch."

"Please. I think, in our little threesome, there were enough bitches to go around."

Francis and my wife were no longer in view. Vicki herself was looking a little fuzzy.

I stood. "Don't call any of us a bitch. I won't have it." My voice was cracking. "I won't have any of this." I threw the scarf at Vicki but my aim was weird or maybe it was just the scarf. It gently descended onto her shoulder, with a fringe falling into her glass. Vicki's smile grew fixed and she raised her arm to motion for a fresh cocktail.

The line to the bathrooms was getting longer and more aggressive. Girls in short high-waist dresses and impractical tops were kicking all five doors.

I stormed to the bathroom. I screamed my name, Francis's and Aviva's names, till the door cracked open and, ignoring the shouts from the line that followed me, I was in.

It was a small bathroom for three people. Pretty quiet too, but for the pounding on the door.

Me, my wife, and Francis. Looking at each other. All three of us smiling, except me and Francis. Francis's belt buckle was undone.

"What the fuck are you doing?"

Aviva was applying lipstick. She seethed through it, "How did that go? You back together with Vicki? If you'd waited another minute I'd probably have had to fuck this trashbag."

"I thought better of it."

Aviva fixed me with a look full of frustrated pity. "That's not really your thing, Sam, thinking better of things. You wanted her to take you back and not give a shit about you and then you'd be free. No adults in the room. An endless bullshit party of baby town abnegation."

I was entirely ignoring Francis and he looked okay with that. I pointed at Aviva and said, "I don't know what that last word means, but I'm not a baby, baby. I'm a man, baby."

Aviva took my finger into her hand and made like she was about to suckle it; an electric charge moved through my parts. Then she jerked it back hard.

I yelped. But she hadn't actually done damage. It was like she used to do, in the last hour of our hours-long fights. I said to Francis. "This is your fault. I can't believe you told Aviva. Is there anything you won't ruin?"

Francis had his hands up. "I'm just doing what I do."

I was seeing double and there were just so many of Francis and Aviva in this bathroom that there was less than one of me, like I was on the ceiling or a stain on the wall.

Francis tried to arrange himself. "Who wants drugs?"

"Give Sam some, maybe that'll straighten him out. Give him some clarity." Aviva was shaking, the lipstick tube looked at about shattering point.

"Sam does not do drugs. Too much not doing them, if you ask me."

The knocking on the bathroom door grew louder and steadier. When it got to double-bass velocity that meant it was a bouncer and we'd have to address it. We had a couple minutes.

"I want to know what the fuck you two are doing," I demanded.

"You haven't any right to ask. None. Francis, if you tell him, I'll stab you in the face."

Francis looked either pained or confused. "We didn't do anything."

Aviva pulled out a cigarette, thought better of it, and threw it back in her purse. "Jesus, Francis, what are you good for?"

"What am I good for? I'm not the bad guy! I never pretended to be anything other than what I am. You two are the ones keeping all those nice people outside waiting. You deserve each other. Someone has to say it and I'm willing to be that brave soul. I'd say there's no need to thank me, but I see now that gratitude is out of fashion."

I yelled at him, "I'd say this is beneath you, but it's not. Nothing is!"

"You're one to talk," Aviva turned on me.

Francis was yelling too: "Really? You fucking coward. And you," he shifted to Aviva, "you clearly won't fight for what's yours. I'm disappointed in both of you."

I had my hand on Francis's hand and I would have punched him, but Aviva beat me to it—she slapped us both in rapid succession, hard. She said, "Fuck you both in the eye, pricks. I'll wear red to your funerals."

She opened the door, body-checked the girl knocking, and slammed the door fast behind her, giving us time to lock. It would be a sec before the knocking started again.

I still had my hand on Francis. I could smell both of our night sweat over the piss and paint of the room. I was tempted to wrestle the drugs from him and throw them away. He saw what I was thinking. Throwing away the drugs would have been dramatic. I wasn't dramatic. I let go of his hand.

Francis put the drugs and his keys in his pocket. When he looked back up his smile was in place.

"So, how'd that go anyway? You and Vicki back together?"

I grabbed his head. The tips of our noses touched and one or both of our breath was wild, in scent and rapidity. "Francis. I think we need a break." I let go of his head too fast so it jerked back and he looked at me like an animal hit by its owner for the first time. I backed out of the bathroom.

A girl immediately went in after me. She was wearing a camouflage parka unzipped over shorts and a Buzzcocks *Singles Going Steady* shirt. She must not have minded Francis because the door didn't reopen.

I didn't want to walk past Vicki again so I headed deeper into the club. There had to be a back way or a window.

The alcove opened up to a larger dance floor. The prints on the wall were obscured by multicolored lights. I felt bad for whoever had done the paintings. All that effort. I saw an exit sign and made a line for it.

1 LOS ANGELES 2016
2 DUBLIN 2013
3 MARRAKECH 2011
4 NEW YORK 2011
5 CHICAGO 2005
6 LOS ANGELES 2011
7 NEW YORK 2011

SEVEN
TIMES
I
WAITED

5

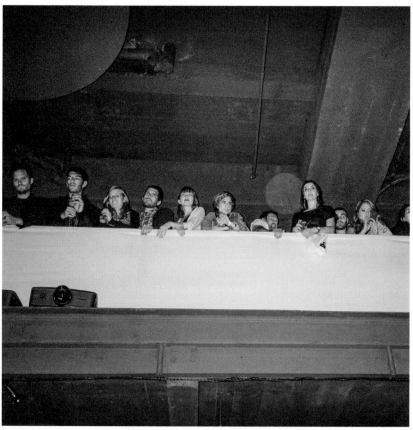

SEVEN BARS
ONE NIGHTCLUB
ONE LOFT
& A DINER

(LAST TIME)

I was very upset and I only had twenty dollars left. My financial and emotional needs converged. I needed a place I could be comforted that would not charge me for drinks. I headed for Pym's.

It was snowing again and the wind was ferocious. I wished I still had the scarf. I wished I had punched Francis. Aviva had looked real good in that bathroom, just inches away from Francis, telling me what for.

It was so cold that I was crying. I was also feeling pretty sorry for myself, so I let the tears have their own distinction. I didn't name them, I just let them be wild and free, origin undetermined. *Oh me*, I thought to myself. I turned my collar up.

My mind was racing or stopping and thinking or doing something, I didn't know. It was so strange seeing Vicki. She wasn't how I'd remembered. I felt a pulverizing disappointment but I was no longer sure what for, and anyway, it wasn't clearly disappointment either, maybe exultation, maybe frostbite.

Aviva had looked tremendous against that sink, lips so close to Francis's and mine. It must have been the lighting. It must have been the lipstick. It often came down to lipstick. She was so angry. I remembered how much I loved when she would be angry at me. She cared so much. You need to really *see* a person to feel that kind of rage.

I opened the door to Pym's and a fist hit my face and there was blood all over the place but, what with the slush, not so you'd notice. A hand pulled me in so I could bleed on the floor. No, not for that purpose. A hand pulled me in so I could get hit again.

My vision already could have been described by a highway patrolman as "blurry." My life did not become more blurry. If there was an opposite of blurry that didn't imply lucidity, that's what was being accomplished right there, with my face being punched.

I saw clearly a fist, repeatedly. I didn't achieve lucidity. I continued to get hit. I was focused on hoping it would stop.

Getting hit once doesn't hurt. It will hurt later and the humiliation may, if psychic weakness is your inclination, last a lifetime, but the blow feels like nothing. Like a newscast on the radio in another room.

Getting hit repeatedly hurts like a motherfucker.

Flannery probably only hit me, truth be told, six or seven times. The back of my head hit a fairly solid wall a couple times, so I think nine or ten is a safe estimate of actual contact with solid mass. By contact number two, I was sober(ish). By contact number five or so, I heard a strange howl from Flannery's direction that sounded like, "COCKSUCKER, WHERE IS MY SCARFFFFFFFF?" By contact number seven, I began to react. I think my hands went up. By nine, my head was jerking back and forth so much that maybe a head butt was in order. By the tenth, Flannery was laid out.

There was blood on my face. I was having a hard time seeing. My hands didn't hurt as much as my face, so I assumed he got felled by lightning or a stray rhino.

"You okay, man?"

Drunk Fireman was standing over Flannery, fists clenching and unclenching. He glanced at me with woozy concern. Sarita and Sanita were on both sides of me dabbing blood from my face.

My mouth felt funny.

"Me? I'm okay. Okay. I'm not sorry at all. You want to know how many regrets I got? You'd need to cut off your hands to count 'em. All your hands." I held up my hands in front of me. I looked at them and then at Flannery lying on the bar floor, moving only the smallest bit. "I sure am strong."

Drunk Fireman and Sanita and Sarita exchanged looks. Drunk Fireman handed me a beer.

I held the beer to my face and shrugged. I smiled until I noticed how much smiling hurt and I stopped. "What happened? Why did that happen? I hate that that happened. Even if I'm glad I killed Flannery. Bye, Flannery. You're a real jerk. Ow."

Sanita said, "Flannery has always hated you, what with your personality and all, but this was craaazzzy. He saw you through the window and just went nuts."

Sarita said from the other side of my face, "I think Sara Seventeen maybe let slip she'd given you the scarf that he'd given Vicki. Dude really loved that scarf. I mean, apparently."

Sanita said, "Oh yeah. That's it. I think I helped him pick it out. Wow. It *was* a pretty great scarf." She shrugged and stepped over Flannery, into the cave of Drunk

Fireman's arms. I couldn't blame her for anything but it felt like I should. Flannery already being unconscious and all. Then something even more terrifying occurred to me.

"Where the fuck is Big Timmy?"

More looks were exchanged. But really, with the dizziness, the blood, skinheads lying on the floor, what were looks?

Drunk Fireman said, "He left. So that's all right. I probably coulda taken him but it would have been real retarded. And this one," he pointed down at Flannery, "Jeezus, what a fucking commotion. Good thing he did all those shots before you showed. Might have hurt you otherwise."

I was drinking the beer, which wasn't helping its cooling effect on my face but was helping to keep me from crying. "Must have been pouring it down his sleeve. Are both my eyes there?"

Sarita checked. "Yes sir. You'll be back on the clocktower in no time."

"Oh good. I got grudges." I kicked Flannery's foot gently. "What do we do with him? I don't want to be around him when he wakes up, but I don't feel like I should have to leave. I have a smooshed face. I need to drink and fill it out."

Drunk Fireman said, "Actually, brother, I think that's going to puff up real nice on its own."

Sarita touched my swelling. "Oh, Sam, ouch. You're going to have an extra couple centimeters of cute."

Sanita curled further into Drunk Fireman and said, "Don't worry, Sam, cute can spare it."

I stepped over Flannery and sat down at the bar. Sanita walked behind the bar and served me. She motioned to the back room. "Virgil's been passed out in the back for the last hour."

"Oh."

"You find Vicki?"

Drunk Fireman pulled Flannery out by one ankle. Sanita poured out four healthy shots of Jameson. When Drunk Fireman came back in, we raised our glasses.

"Up with us, down with them."

We slammed the glasses down. Drunk Fireman didn't seem that drunk, actually. He was one of those types who got more sober when he drank. Maybe I'd ask him for a ride home.

I said, "Anyone seen Aviva?"

They exchanged looks again.

1 NEW YORK 2002
2 PARIS 2004
3 NEW ORLEANS 2010
4 NEW YORK 2012
5 NEW YORK 1999
6 NEW YORK 2012
7 NEW YORK 1999

SEVEN
MOMENTS
OF
CLARITY

2

SEVEN BARS
ONE NIGHTCLUB
ONE LOFT
& A DINER

10

How long is a marriage supposed to last? I mean, being realistic. When I was a teenager, I didn't want to get married at all. When I was twenty-one, I wanted to get married young and be divorced by thirty, so that I'd be someone who believed in true love when I was young and then wised up. When I met Aviva, I thought all my ideas had changed and I wanted to be married forever.

When I first moved in with Aviva, we had already broken up twice, woken up so often to broken glass that we threw out the rugs. We knew each other's moves so well it was like dancing, which neither of us did with other people. She said, "This is nice. Now we can keep an eye on each other."

When I saw Aviva in the window of Odessa, the Ukrainian restaurant, she was not alone.

The slush had made a slippery banana of Avenue A and I was soaked. I had told myself that I was just taking the long way to the train, maybe to sober up, maybe to take in the winter air, maybe to by chance pass by where I had been told my wife had gone to eat. They hadn't mentioned that she might have company.

Big Timmy. My wife. A plate of pierogies. She looked tired and happy. Sour cream and apple sauce always made her happy.

Fuck it, Big Timmy wasn't anything but a man, and a pierogi ain't nothing but a dumpling. I went in.

I shook myself off before getting to their table. They saw me coming. They were either really digging in or were doing a silent communication over the table. I had a small window of opportunity before decisions were going to be made for me.

"Aviva. Timothy."

Big Timmy didn't look at me. He said to Aviva, "Your call, lady. Just say the word."

"He's my husband," she replied. She shrugged like she couldn't help it. Electricity ran through me. She registered how dinged-up I was.

I said, "In a better world, it would have happened over you."

Big Timmy saw my face too. He stood up. I put my hand on a fork.

"Tim," I said, "you know and I know you can kill me, but that's my wife. I'll do something permanent to you before I go down."

A couple waiters were watching but they were used to late-night standoffs. There was at least a girl with us to cover the check.

Tim said, "You are worthless. Someday she's gonna know that. Someday everybody's gonna know that. I hope Flannery did that to you cuz you fucking deserve it." He inhaled deeply and it felt like he was taking breath directly from my lungs. He exhaled and I felt napkins flutter behind me. With a tectonic shift, Big Timmy said, "Fuck this noise," and walked away. The door slammed behind him and the waitstaff looked relieved. I collapsed into the booth.

Aviva gathered all the napkins from the table and dipped them in ice water. She came and sat on my side of the booth and dabbed my face.

"Sanita and Sarita texted me. About Flannery. They were so excited."

"I'm pretty sure I didn't do anything."

"Duh, Sam. Obviously. But like everyone else in this stupid town, Drunken Fireman thinks you're the cat's pajamas. He's telling everyone you took Flannery out with one punch."

I winced. "I'm not sure he's really thinking that one through."

"Probably not. But you buy him drinks and don't treat him like a Pegasus cuz he's a fireman and you don't treat him like a leper just cuz he's basically a cop with a lot of dead friends. You treat him like you treat everyone." She licked some sour cream off her spoon. "Of course, it's a bit problematic when you treat your wife like a man, but I guess that's something else. We don't need to get into all that."

I said, "We aren't as much husband and wife as other husbands and wives are, I know that."

Aviva pulled out a small bottle of whiskey and, not bothering to hide it, tilted it over her mouth.

I went on, "But I think we do have a bond that a lot of couples don't have . . ."

"A lot of couples are dead, sure."

"I'm being serious. Tonight has made me think a lot . . ."

Aviva pointed a dumpling at me. "Tonight, where you spent the entire night chasing after that prissy bitch."

"But you were always on my mind."

Aviva laughed. "Yeah, because I was in half the places you went. I had a bit of a night myself. Not that anyone's asking."

"Yeah, see? You were always there. And I want to hear all about it."

It was crazy how the bright diner lights made Aviva even more desirable. Maybe it was the dried sweat from all the night's troubles or the fact that there was no darkness to hide the rips and tears on her black ensemble. Or maybe I just liked the lines under her eyes and the way she wore her mascara and eyeliner, and I liked her face. It was a face that could carry a lot, one I knew that I could breathe around, late at night and early in the morning.

I told her I really liked her face and waited for her to stop laughing.

"Do you remember when we first met, how awkward you were?" I asked her.

"I wasn't awkward, you were boring."

Her leg was against mine. It wasn't rubbing but it was against mine and it wasn't being pulled away.

"I meant to show you the photo book. They printed that picture of Virgil at Tompkins."

"I know all about that, Sam. I hooked that shit up. Editor used to work for me. I was at his loft when he was doing the final selection. But you were already in the running. It's important you know that, Sam. Like, really know it."

"Thank you, Aviva. God, I held that book at crazy angles on the train so people could see what I was in." I paused. "I'm thinking of getting a digital camera. You know, see what happens."

"I feel like I may have suggested that before."

"It's possible that I've been a bit wrong about a number of things. Tremendously, egregiously wrong. Like, wrong in a way that would make a stupid man blush. Wrong in a way that *Sorry* doesn't cover. Though I swear that apologies and groveling and true contrition coupled with a complete overhaul of actions and worldview, are in the offering. Whether they're accepted or not. I have been wrong—stupidly, cruelly wrong, like it's a job. Not for nothing, I'd like to be wrong less."

Aviva said, "Speaking for the world at large, I think we'd all like that."

I smiled at her through drying blood and expanding flesh. "I want to go home. I'm tired."

"Okay, Sam. You can sleep on top of the covers."

I nodded.

"I'm a bit gakked out, so I may need you to go down on me so I can sleep."

I nodded again.

I moved out of the booth and threw my last twenty down. My wife took care of the tip.

I put out my arm.

Aviva, as if from muscle memory, took it.

I went home with my wife, who loves me.

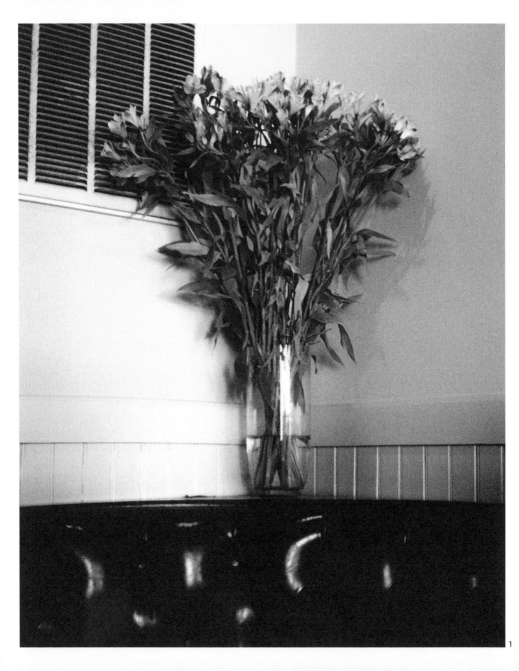

ONE

TIME

WE

GOT

BACK

TOGETHER

1 TIVOLI, NY 1998
2 LONDON 2012

NICK ZINNER plays guitar in the three-time Grammy-nominated band Yeah Yeah Yeahs
and hardcore group Head Wound City. His photos have been published in four previous
books, as well as in the *New York Times, Vice*, and *Rolling Stone*. He has exhibited in
solo shows in Tokyo, Berlin, New York, London, Los Angeles, and Mexico City.

ZACHARY LIPEZ lives in New York City, where he has tended bar for the last twenty
years. He is a regular contributor to *Noisey*, and his music and culture writing have also
appeared in *Vice, Hazlitt, Pitchfork, Bandcamp Daily, Talkhouse, Inc.*, and *Penthouse*.

STACY WAKEFIELD'S artist books, published for many years under the imprint Evil Twin,
have been collected by institutions including the Museum of Modern Art in New York
and London's Tate Modern. She runs a studio dedicated solely to book design and
production. Her first novel, *The Sunshine Crust Baking Factory*, was published by
Akashic in 2015. She lives in the Catskills and Brooklyn.

PUBLISHED BY AKASHIC BOOKS
PHOTOGRAPHS ©2018 NICK ZINNER
TEXT ©2018 ZACHARY LIPEZ
DESIGNED AND EDITED BY STACY WAKEFIELD

ISBN: 978-1-61775-667-2
LIBRARY OF CONGRESS CONTROL NUMBER: 2018931231

PRINTED IN CHINA
FIRST PRINTING

AKASHIC BOOKS
BROOKLYN, NEW YORK, USA
BALLYDEHOB, CO. CORK, IRELAND
TWITTER: @AKASHICBOOKS
FACEBOOK: AKASHICBOOKS
EMAIL: INFO@AKASHICBOOKS.COM
WEBSITE: WWW.AKASHICBOOKS.COM